The Stroke of Midnight: A Fairytale Romance

First Edition

By Serenity Sky

Published in 2022 by
Ballads & Bards Bookhouse

Ballads & Bards Bookhouse
Wonnarua Country
AUSTRALIA
www.balladsandbardsbookhouse.com

A catalogue record of this work is available from the National Library of Australia

The Stroke of Midnight: A Fairytale Romance
ISBN: 978 0 6454389 1 8 (paperback)

10 9 8 7 6 5 4 3 2 1

Cover Design
Nabin Karna
Text Design
Istvan Szabo
Editor
Dr Danny Decillis

Printed by Ingram Spark, an Ingram Industries company, and Kindle Direct Printing, an Amazon company.

Ballads & Bards Bookhouse acknowledges the Traditional Owners of the country on which we work, the Wonnarua and Awabakal nations, and recognises their continuing connection to their land, waters and culture. We pay respects to their Elders past, present and emerging.

Dedicated to my B...
Never could I have achieved this without you
No one could have supported me
the way you have
Now is the time to see YOU soar...
I love you

TABLE OF CONTENTS

Prologue

It was storming the day she died. Victoria Baron had had been ill for many months, and the mansion held its breath with her in her final moments. When finally her chest stilled and her eyes closed for the last time, Arina, the maid, let out a great despairing wail for her lost mistress, as Digby Baron laid his head on his wife's hand and wept.

Out in the hall, Asche listened to the cries of her father and the staff. She sat by the bay window that sat directly across the hallway from the doors that led into the grande master suite. It was dark outside the window, save for when the lightning lit the sky. Asche watched the rain falling as she listened to the rumbling of the thunder above her and the weeping of the people on the other side of the door.

Asche's life was to change with the death of her mother. Despite her tender age, she knew this, but she had never dreamed the changes that were to come would come as drastically as they did.

"Be kind, my precious girl," her mother had told her in the days gone past, when she would sit for hours at a time reading to her as she lay in the bed, too sickly to move. It was something Asche had been grateful for, to be told that whatever illness her mother fought, it was not contagious and therefore, she was able to be in there with her for what time she had left.

"I will, Mother," she had answered. "I will be kind, always."

And kind she was... When Arina would rap her knuckles with a yardstick when she lost her train of thought during lessons; when her father, in his grief, would throw things across the room; when she would be in town and get scolded by the women for running in her dress, or when children would laugh and taunt her for being unkempt when her clothes would become dirty or torn and Arina didn't notice for a few days; through it all she remained kind. Kind she remained even when her father finally remarried and her stepmother regarded her with disdain, her stepsisters bullied her and they saw her well worn clothing as an excuse to keep her that way; directing her to cook and clean, leaving her dresses dirtier and more torn than ever, and when they began to call her... Cinderella.

1

Asche was on her hands and knees, scrubbing the kitchen floor in the basement of the mansion. A large fire was blazing in the grate, readying the porridge for breakfast; it was the only light in the kitchen as the sun had yet to rise.

Between the heat of the summer morning, the fire needed for breakfast and the physical exertion of cleaning the stone floor, Asche had sweat running down her face and back. She had discarded her skirts entirely. It was why she was up so early. It was too hot during the day to have the fire burning or do any excessive cleaning, so she rose before dawn to make breakfast and do the harder chores in her underclothes while no one was awake.

Only once had she been caught, and luckily Arina, the head housekeeper now, took great humour in finding her in her incredibly indecent state of undress. "Lucky it was me, Love! And no' Gerry!" she had laughed raucously. "Wha' a state you would 'ave 'ad 'im in then, eh?"

Arina's husband Gerry was the Baron family yardman, so he was often up early seeing to the horses. "I know when Gerry is awake, Arina," Asche had answered breathlessly, her heart racing at being caught almost naked. "He opens the chicken coop and the rooster starts crowing. I *always* have enough time to get dressed before he brings the eggs in."

"I should 'ope so!"

There was no chance of that happening today. Asche gazed through the split barn style door that looked out into the yard beyond the kitchen. The sky was finally starting to lighten. No crowing rooster. The carriage had lost a wheel the previous weekend, so Gerry was spending his days in town collecting materials and working on the repair. This was not possible to do in the dark when all the smiths and carpenters were closed, so he had been sleeping in of late.

Asche scrubbed away at the last section of the floor, right by the door. When she finally finished, she leaned back on her heels and surveyed her work. "Quite adequate," she huffed, wiping the sweat from her forehead and getting to her feet.

Asche stirred the pot over the fire. The porridge was the perfect consistency. She took the pot from the fire, replacing it with the black iron kettle filled with water, and placed the porridge on the bench. Once Asche had climbed back into her dress, a simple grey frock with a white scalloped apron, she then opened the rest of the door, the bottom half that had remained latched while she cleaned, so she could enter the yard and release the chickens, immediately triggering the rooster, who began to crow just as a loud clock chimed in the distance.

Asche looked towards the sound. There, far in the distance, peeking through the top of the thick green trees that separated her family's land from the rest of the city, was the palace clock tower. Only the tops of the towers could be seen from the yard, but from her room in the attic, she could see the whole palace.

She had spent many an early morning gazing out her window, fantasising about the lives of the people who must live there; lords and ladies, the King and his Queen, the Princes and Princess; what she would do in order to be among them for just one day... away from the life that had been so cruelly thrust upon her from the day her father returned home that day with her stepmother.

Contessa Georgina LaBelle was the proudest woman Asche had ever met in her life. She had lost her husband during the war and despite her best efforts, her daughters were not the highest desired prizes of the royal court. She was tall, with long black hair that was always coiffed to perfection. Her eyes were almost as black as her hair, sitting either side of a symmetrical nose on her perfectly powdered face.

Every gown she owned was of the highest quality, and she only ever wore them three times; once for the fitting, once for the purchase, and once for the event itself. Then it was handed down to Asche's stepsisters for them to spend the next two weeks squabbling over who got to wear it first.

Her face, while beautiful, held a hateful sneer almost all of the time. It only changed when Asche's father would return from his business trips. It was the only sign of her humanity, her ability to feel anything else but disgust for the life she had; pain for what she had lost.

Asche kept this in mind with every unkind word, with every barked order, with every harsh tone; that everyone was the sum of their experiences, and she could not possibly understand what her stepmother had been through. This was something that had only come to her as she grew from a teenager into an adult. As a child, it was much harder, for she was still reeling from the pain of her own loss, as well as attempting to navigate the new family her father had created and the new role they had forced upon her.

Asche collected the eggs from the henhouse and made her way back to the kitchen just as the first rays of sunlight shone through the trees and the bells started ringing. She quickly crossed to the fire and removed the iron kettle, placing it beside the porridge pot.

Each and every morning was the same. Asche would clean while the fires steadily prepared the breakfast. Once the cleaning was finished and breakfast was prepared she would take everything upstairs with Arina to the grand dining room. The family only ever ate there, never in the smaller, more appropriate dining room that was still more than appropriate for standard meals; Georgina would never allow herself or her daughters to live in any manner less than the best that was available, and her father was sure to see she received it.

His Honourable Sir, Conte Digby Baron, was a highly respected man in the city. He was tall, with broad shoulders and light brown hair. His eyes were blue; warm but always sad. Despite being counted amongst royal circles, even having been knighted himself by His Royal Majesty King Hugo IV himself for his role in the war, he held a day job as a Magistrate's Justice of the Peace. Many had told him it was unnecessary, for surely he did not need to *work*, a man of such stature?

Asche knew why... Her father was wracked with terrible guilt over the loss of her mother and subsequent treatment of Asche by his new wife and stepdaughters, but he so greatly feared being left all alone that he dared not speak out about their treatment of her. And so, he busied himself with his work, not only so he would not be home to bear witness to his daughter being treated horrendously, but so he could feel better that he was doing some good in the world by settling disputes between the people of the city and locking away criminals who would see them harmed.

Asche reached the top of the stairs and stepped into the main foyer of the mansion, crossing the green tiles in front of the sweeping staircase to the dining room opposite, placing the large tray on the table and laying out the place settings.

Her stepsisters came in just as she was ladling the porridge into bowls, ignoring her with resolute purpose. June was older by two years. She had blonde hair that was curled and pinned back onto the top of her head, giving an extra half a foot of height. Her eyes were an icy blue and her skin was flawless. She carried the same constant sneer on her face as her mother, and she never looked Asche in the eye when she made her demands.

Charlotte however, did. She still directed Asche as she pleased, but she often seemed apologetic about it, sad looks on her face and never speaking to her harshly. She was shorter than her mother and sister. Her hair was the same colour as her mother's, and she always wore it down, with side the sides pinned back practically as to prevent it from falling in her face.

Unlike her sister, her face had a smattering of freckles across her nose. Contessa Georgina often scolded her for them, for every time another appeared, her mother knew that she had once again been roaming the city in the sunshine, for whatever else could cause such blemishes to the skin?

June would *never*. She spent her time indoors, at luncheons and charity dinners, consorting with all the right people and only placing herself at the right events, as an heir *should*, and Charlotte should be looking to her sister as an example for appropriate behaviour; so said Contessa Georgina.

Today they were all off to yet another such event. June was in a royal blue velvet gown, with many layers bolstering her skirts and large trailing sleeves, while Charlotte was wearing a simple yellow dress with three quarter sleeves ending in lace.

When Georgina entered on the arm of her father, she was wearing a blood red silken gown with a large bustle at the back and fur trim, her shoulders bare due to the low sleeve. "Cinderella," she greeted Asche with a nod, not looking her in the eye as her father pulled out her chair and she took it graciously.

"Good morning, Daughter," her father said, smiling at her. He had long since stopped responding to his wife and stepdaughter's use of the name. It was possible he did not even notice it anymore. He never used it himself, though he also only ever referred to her as "Daughter".

"Good morning, Father," she smiled back, placing his tea and porridge before him, before making her way around the table and serving the others.

"Mornin' everyone!" a bright, cheery voice rang out.

"Good morning, Arina! How did you sleep?" Digby asked just as brightly.

"Does she *have* to be so loud this early in the morning?" June sighed, placing a finger to her temple.

"Off you go, Lass," Arina mumbled to her as she passed. Asche nodded and quietly slipped back through to the foyer and back down to the kitchen.

Now was the time she had to eat for herself, just a few minutes until the dining room would then need to be cleared. She sat at the back door, eating her own cold portion of the porridge, thinking that at least while her father was at work that day, her stepmother and stepsisters would not be around to make the most of his absence.

2

Far away, on the other side of the city, in the royal palace, King Hugo was mourning, as the anniversary of his wife's death arrived. He was gazing out of the window in very much the same way Asche was wont to do, with longing.

Much like Digby Baron, he was desperate for his family to remain whole and happy. He had lost much family to the war almost two decades ago, becoming one of only two survivors in all his family, the other being his younger brother Edward. Then he had spent the years that followed rebuilding his country, his people, and his family, marrying his beautiful Queen Roberta and raising his three precious children.

Queen Roberta was beloved by the people of their kingdom, by her children, and most of all by King Hugo. She had brought him back from the depression that had set upon him after suffering through the front line of war. He was not the immediate heir to the kingdom, but when he lost both his father, the King Unos, and his brother, Prince Raolo, the duty fell to him. Queen Roberta had seen him through the pain of his grief, and now without her, it had returned tenfold.

King Hugo watched the children play in the courtyard from the window. They were his brother Edward's grandchildren. He was incredibly jealous of Edward, to have such sparks of light in his life as he did not. Edward only had one daughter, Princess Bodelia, but already he had *three* grandchildren!

Of his three children, Princess Zarina was the only one to have prospects, but she seemed content to keep them at a distance while she cooped herself up in the library reading every book in sight. She paid particular attention to the ones about political relations and government business.

Zarina had been conceived within a year of the war ending and her father marrying Roberta, and she was insistent, even more so since the death of her mother, that war would never again threaten her family and her kingdom. "I may never be Queen, Father!" she said told him. "But a diplomat and an ambassador to the crown I will forever remain and if Sebastian is to be named King, then I will be making sure he does not undo all of your hard work by doing something stupid!" she had railed.

Sebastian, his elder son and heir to the throne of the kingdom, was a serious young man and a great source of pride to King Hugo. His strong visage held firm for his family while they mourned their wife and mother, and indeed the whole kingdom as they mourned their Queen.

While a gentleman, he was still young and could be a bit of a rogue when the situation called for it. Travels with his friends, lying in until midday after long, decadent and somewhat hedonistic nights; he had certainly given the family cause to be somewhat doubtful in the past.

He had however, proven that he was the backbone of the family, and seeing his behaviour during the loss of Queen Roberta was what made King Hugo all the more certain that Sebastian was ready for the throne, and would do right by the kingdom when the time came.

Despite this occasional showing of integrity and responsibility, a ragamuffin with love and ladies he remained. He had still not married or provided King Hugo with what he desired most, a large family he could spend the rest of his days loving and spoiling.

His younger son was no better or worse in that sense. Vladimir was not the man his brother was, with the parties and the philandering, but he was just as fun loving and fanciful. He was far happier to spend time running about the city and getting caught up with all likes of town folk from bakers and blacksmiths to travelling circus performers and singers. He filled his days revelling in all the kingdom had to offer, as opposed to Sebastian, who only revelled between the legs of whoever took his fancy that day.

King Hugo decided he was going to put a stop to it. He was the *King* and he would see to it that he got exactly what he desired. "JARVIS!" he called roughly.

"Yes, Your Majesty?" a small reedy voice responded immediately.

"Summon Sebastian at once," he ordered, not looking away from the window and the children playing in the courtyard below.

♠

"Yes, my Lord, *oh!*"

Sebastian's latest catch was rather vocal, more so than he was used to, but he found it helped. As the woman's naked body heaved with every thrust, forcing another loud moan from her lips, Sebastian found himself hardening even further, if that were at all possible. He reached forward, cupping one of her supple breasts in his hand, eliciting another moan from her and another throb from his phallus.

He was close. He pulled his manhood out of the red headed maiden just long enough to drag her forward on the bed and roll her onto her stomach. She let out a squeal of delight that made his ears ring as he slid back into her wet folds, increasing his speed as he gripped her curved hips from behind.

He threw himself forward, a groan escaping his lips, his load releasing with such force as to exhaust him immediately. He closed his eyes, trying to catch his breath, both his and the woman's body beneath him heaving in synchronicity as the tingling of his body began to lessen.

"Oh, Your Highness!" the maiden panted, raising her head and pulling her hair from her face. Sebastian stepped back, bending down to pull his pants from his ankles back to his waist. "I could spend all my life doing *just* this!"

"Not possible, fair maiden!" he answered breathlessly. "Enid, was it?"

"Eleanor, Sire," she said uncertainly, drawing up her dress to cover herself.

"Yes, well Eleanor, see, *I* am going to be King, and as such I will have far greater responsibilities to be filling my days with than this," Sebastian said simply as he did up his pants.

"To be sure, Your Highness, but you will need a Queen, will you not?"

"Indeed I will," Sebastian answered, smoothing back his hair. "But there are certain expectations of *her* also," he winked, before heading for the door. "Be a dear and get yourself dressed? I shall send in Marguerite to help and see you out."

The Prince heard her start to protest, but it was cut off as the door closed and he turned away from it... only to come face to face with the Viscount. "Your Highness! Good morning!"

"A good morning it is indeed, Jarvis!" Sebastian answered cheerily, taking his arm and leading him back down the hallway. "Whatever can I do for you, good Sir?"

"The King wishes to see you, Sire," the Viscount informed him, regarding Prince Sebastian curiously, looking back towards his door.

"Oh? Whatever for?"

"He did not say," the Viscount answered dryly, an eyebrow raised. "But I have a feeling it involves whomsoever you have in your room."

Prince Sebastian looked away sheepishly.

"Father, we have discussed this," Prince Sebastian was telling King Hugo. "I will absolutely meet my obligations to the crown *when I am wearing it*, but in the meantime I maintain the right to certain freedoms! I do not wish to settle for any noble maiden that you present simply because you insist on grandchildren!"

"I understand you do not wish to settle, nor would I expect any future King to do so," King Hugo said. "And I do remember our bargain that you would be required to have an appropriate Queen only when you were to be crowned King."

"Then why summon me?" Sebastian was confused. "If you want grandchildren so badly, why not find an adequate match for Zarina?" he suggested. "Surely that would be far easier and as the eldest, a marriage for her is far more appropriate than arranging a marriage for a younger sibling, heir or no?"

"I would agree with you, but Zarina is adamant on having a family only once you take the throne also," King Hugo sighed, rubbing his forehead.

"Why?"

"She insists your early reigning years will be a transition period for you and the entire kingdom and she does not want to be hindered in helping you due to childbearing duties she will have to her husband," the King answered. "She also thinks that should issues arise with other kingdoms then having an eligible sister prepared for marriage may be a political move that is needed. In this, I agree with her."

Sebastian nodded thoughtfully. His sister was ever considerate. He appreciated her loyalty and commitment to his future reign more than he could express. "Wait," he suddenly said. "When did you discuss this? My reign may not come for decades, Father? She cannot possibly put off marriage indefinitely?"

"We discussed it while he waited for you. She just left," King Hugo said. "And you are quite right; she certainly cannot wait for an undefined period of time." Sebastian nodded, pleased his father was seeing sense. "However, the defined period of time has been decided and the terms agreed upon between she, myself and the Viscount. Your sister will be betrothed within the year, provided the choice of match is hers and that it is directly beneficial to the crown and kingdom."

"A *year?*" Sebastian exclaimed. "But you said she would not marry until I was crowned? How long could her engagement possibly be?"

"Therein lies my announcement and why I summoned you here," his father said, rising from his chair and coming around his desk. "In three days there is to be a ball; a ball that *every* eligible maiden, be she commoner, nobility or royal, from all four corners of the continent; will attend. At that ball, you will have your selection for a bride-"

"-But Father! You *just said-*"

"-I *said* that you would not be required to marry until you are crowned," the King cut him off. "And nor will you be. That is why in a *week from today*, there will be a coronation, where you and your bride will be named King and Queen."

Sebastian was shocked. He struggled to regain his composure. "But... but Father, you are still *alive!* You are not sick, are you?" he began to ramble. "Why ever would you abdicate?"

"Because I am *old*, Son–"

"–Father, you are *barely* grey," Sebastian frowned.

"Even so," the King said gently. "I have seen and experienced things that make me far older than my age, my boy. I have not been the same since I lost your mother, and I do find myself longing day after day for things I may not have until I am too old to appreciate and enjoy them.

"Not only that, but the kingdom deserves a King who can provide what they need; joy, growth, innovation. It is time for fresh blood, and surely you will appreciate coming into your Kingship with me still alive rather than having passed! Think of all the guidance I could provide you from here rather than from the grave!" At this, King Hugo gave a hearty chuckle. Sebastian remained frozen from the shock. "First, the ball; next, the coronation!" Sebastian swallowed hard, not meeting his father's eyes.

3

As it so happened, Contessa Georgina LaBelle-Baron and her pair of daughters left plenty to keep Asche busy while they were away, so much so that she barely had the opportunity to appreciate the time to herself. "Do not forget that we are hosting a meeting of the Queen Roberta Remembrance Charity League tomorrow, so be sure polish the silver *and* the floors," she had told Asche as she put on her gloves in readiness of leaving for the luncheon. "And certainly don't forget to scrub down the balcony and place the furniture. Then, the carpets need cleaning and the bakery order needs to be put in."

"Oh, Mother, the little iced cakes?" June piped up, placing her hat delicately atop her tower of curls. "And the cheese tarts? We simply *must* have the cheese tarts. Baroness Claudette of Shaw *loves* them!"

"Excellent idea, June, very good," Georgina said. "Be sure to make sure the tarts are on the list, as well as the iced cakes and the standard luncheon order. *Then* go to the Bier's manor and let them know we will require additional help if they are willing to send their maids whilst Lord Bier is at court tomorrow."

"Yes Stepmother; everything will be perfect, I promise."

Georgina looked Asche up and down critically. "See that it is, Cinderella." The three made their way through the front door, where Gerry was waiting with the finally repaired carriage. "Oh, and Cinderella?" she called over her shoulder.

"Yes, Stepmother?"

"...Do not forget the windows," she smiled, before climbing into the carriage. June sneered and rolled her eyes before following suit. Charlotte just gave her a small, sad wave.

The windows alone had taken most of the morning. Once the sun had reached its zenith, Asche started the carpets, to ensure they had the best chance of drying quickly without leaving a damp smell once the sun had gone down. It was during these specific tasks that she was actually grateful for the summer heat.

The bakery order had to come next on her list, or she risked not getting it in on time. "You, 'op to it Lass!" Arina had told her. "Heidi an' me'll sor' the balcony while you're gone!"

"Thank you, Arina!" Asche had said, grateful to not have to rush through town, risking mistakes, in order to get the remaining chores finished. Arina had been doing that for many, many years now. She, Heidi and Gerry all had their specific chores, while anything extra was always directed to Asche. Arina had made a point of making a big deal about 'everythin' I 'ave to do' and ''ow busy I am each day' to ensure her chores list never grew. That way, when the Contessa leaned heavily on Asche with additional work, Arina and Heidi could take some of it off her hands without her knowing.

Asche wandered through town at a leisurely pace, enjoying the light breeze and moments of shade as she passed under the trees that lined the streets. When she reached the bakery, a tinkling bell announced her presence.

"Good afternoon Asche!" Gregor piped up from the back room, waving from the doorway with flour on his little face and pink mush all over his pudgy little hands.

"Good afternoon!" she called back, laughing. "What is that you have got all over you? Where is your mother? I have an order for the Contessa's meeting tomorrow!"

"It's icing!" he announced proudly, grinning. "I'm doing my first cupcakes!"

"And *I* am right here!" Greta answered, coming into the shop, covered in flour and wiping her hands on her apron. "How are you, Asche?"

"Very well, thank you Greta," Asche said. "I have the list for the Women's Charity League meeting tomorrow." She handed over the list.

"This is quite a list!" Greta exclaimed. "It'll cost her!"

"Well, you know she has it," Asche sighed. "Will you be able to do everything by tomorrow?"

Greta pulled her glasses from her pocket and exclaimed the list. "Yes... Yes I believe so. Shan't be a problem, my dear! I'll see that it gets done."

"Wonderful!" Asche exhaled in relief.

"Pick up around eleven?"

"Perfect. Thank you Greta!" Asche said. "Goodbye Gregor!"

"Bye, bye!"

Asche stepped back out into the warm summer sunshine. One task down, one to go; she was about to head in the direction of home, when there was a loud trumpet coming from the city centre. She started, startled at the noise, turning towards it expectantly.

Riding up on white chargers was a royal guard, accompanied by none other than the Viscount's right hand man, the Marquis Winston Harvey of Trellis. "HEAR YE, HEAR YE!" he was calling to the growing crowd. "*Make it known that in two days hence, there is to be a festival, lasting three days, in honour of His Majesty, the Crown Prince Sebastian Reginald Hubert Matthew Bishop the Seventh!*" The crowd started chattering excitedly.

"*On the third day, the Prince will choose for himself a bride and Queen of our kingdom! As such, our beloved King, his Royal Highness King Hugo*

Cuthbert Phillipe Bartholomew Frederic Bishop the Fourth, declares that every maiden, regardless of station, is invited to attend!"

The crowd exploded with noise. Asche stood rooted to the spot, shocked at the announcement as the people around her yelled and cried out in amazement at the plans for the festival. When she finally came to her senses, she made her way through town back to the sprawling manors and mansions of the eastern side of the city where she lived, running the whole way.

Asche arrived on the front step of the Lord Bier's manor, breathless and sweaty. She pulled the cord by the front door and heard a ringing bell disappearing into the distance. The door was answered in less than ten seconds by a short blonde maid in a navy dress. "Good afternoon Mistress Asche," she greeted Asche formally. "Whatever can the house of Bier do for you this fine day? Dear? Are-are you quite alright?"

"Oh yes! Good afternoon Mistress Delia," Asche responded in kind, puffing from the exertion. "I have been sent by the Contessa... to-to request that yourself and Kathleen join-join the Women's Charity League meeting tomorrow?" Asche took a deep breath and exhaled slowly, regaining herself. "There will be many in attendance and Contessa Georgina fears there will not be enough hands."

"I do not believe we have any other engagements," Delia said thoughtfully, watching Asche with interest. "Lord Bier is away tomorrow at the royal court, so he shan't require us here. You can inform the Contessa we shall assist," she nodded.

"Oh, thank you very much Delia!" Asche said. "Have-have you heard the news?"

"No Dear? What news?" Delia asked with wide eyes.

"There is to be a festival! At the palace!"

"A *festival*? At the *palace*?" Delia cried out mockingly, hand on her heart. "Whatever will they think of next!"

"No," Asche laughed. "No, you don't understand! The Prince is to select a bride!"

"A *bride*?" Delia gasped. "That *is* news!"

"That is not all!" Asche rushed on hurriedly. "By the King's orders *every* maiden is invited to attend *regardless of their station!*"

"What are you saying, Child?" Delia said, frowning.

"The Prince is able to choose from anyone, Delia. They needn't be royalty or nobility!" Asche explained. "He could marry *Kathleen* if he so chose!"

"You are saying that we are *invited* to the *palace* for a *festival*?" she asked deliberately slowly.

"YES!" Asche squealed excitedly. Suddenly the clock tower struck two thirty, and Asche was immediately drained of her excitement. "The Contessa will return by three! I must go!" She dashed back down the front steps. "Tell everyone!" she called back to Delia. "Everyone must know!"

Asche ran the whole way home, cutting through the trees at the back of the mansion property line, just making it through the back door of the kitchen as Gerry pulled the carriage around, returning with her stepmother and stepsisters.

"Tha' was close!" Arina exclaimed. "I didn' think you would make i' back!"

"I would never do that to you, Arina," Asche said, kissing her on the cheek, before quickly arranging her hair and wiping her sweaty face on her apron. She then took the tea tray from Arina and forced herself to breathe normally as she climbed the stairs.

Instead of passing the staircase into the dining room, she took a left and carried the tray into the conservatory, where sat the Contessa Georgina, June and Charlotte. "Good afternoon stepmother; stepsisters; how was your luncheon?"

"Boring," Charlotte answered immediately, getting an immediate deadly look from her mother.

"If you made the effort to involve yourself properly, you may not find it so!" June snapped. "I make such efforts to get you in with the right crowds, only to have you sit there and *embarrass* me!"

"Quite so," Georgina said. "Charlotte, you would do well to thank your sister and be *grateful!* We have a name to uphold! If you ever wish to find an appropriate match for marriage then you need to present yourself in the right manner!"

"Oh! Marriage!" Asche gasped, almost dropping the tray. She regained her balance and slid the tray onto the table.

"Do watch what you are doing, Cinderella!" Georgina sighed, folding up her fan.

"I am so sorry," Asche said, flustered. "You just reminded me of the announcement! It is very exciting!"

"What is exciting?" June asked. "What announcement?"

"You... you did not hear while you were at the luncheon?" Asche asked. "People all over the city heard the news this afternoon. I heard when I went to the bakery to place the order for tomorrow."

"Well what announcement, Girl?" Georgina snapped. "Spit it out!"

"Oh, yes! Of course, forgive me Stepmother. The Marquis of Trellis was in the city today, telling everyone that there will be a festival starting the day after tomorrow that will last three whole days-"

"-A festival!" June gasped. "Lasting three days? Think of all the gowns, Mother!"

"That's not all!" Asche went on. "It will be at the pala-!"

"-The palace?" Charlotte repeated, eyes wide, her hands covering her mouth. "There has not been an event there since-"

"-Since the Queen died," Contessa Georgina cut her off. "This is marvellous news, Girls!"

"That is still not all!" Asche said, pouring tea from the pot into the three delicate teacups where they sat on their saucers.

"Well, then, get on with it!" Georgina said harshly.

"The festival is in honour of the Prince-" This time there was no interruption. "-And he is going to choose a bride!"

The sounds that exploded from the three women was greater than what she had experienced on the street. The squealing alone was enough to make neighbourhood dogs howl. Asche smiled, unable to help herself at their joy.

"Mother, do you know what this *means*-?"

"-Mother, why would the Prince be choosing a bride now?"

"Oh! Girls, I shall see to it that you both erode all competition with your very presence-!"

"-But he is not even King yet-?"

"-Oh, but he *will* be and now I shall be Queen-!"

"-*Yes!* Yes, my dear, I will see to it that you are-!"

"-Why does it take three days to select a bride-?"

"-Mother, we must get to the seamstress immediately-!"

"-No, we must organise a hairstylist! They book out faster-!"

"-Oh, you are right! But we must also ensure our dresses are perfect-!"

"-*And* we cannot forget about all of the other preparations-!"

"-The meeting tomorrow-!"

"-CINDERELLA!" they all cried out.

"Yes?" Asche said, straightening her back. "What can I do?"

"Go to the seamstress and order the ball gowns-!"

"–No, get to the hairstylist and book us in for *all three days*–!"

"–First get Gerry to add golden embellishments to the carriage–!"

"–But there are three days of the festival, we cannot wear the same thing each day–!"

"–Definitely *not!* We shall need three dresses *each*–!"

"–And while every single one must be glorious, each night's should look better than the day before–!"

"–YES! CINDERELLA *GO!*"

4

"Every invitation must be addressed and delivered *today*, Jarvis!" King Hugo was ordering the Viscount. "Done and done, Sire!" Jarvis responded. "The Marquis has made the announcements throughout the city and every invitation for our kingdom has been received with not a single unanswered response!"

"And the other kingdoms?"

"The closer kingdoms have responded, sharing their joy for the upcoming marriage, Your Highness!" Viscount Jarvis said happily. "The messengers are still returning from the outer kingdoms."

"Very good," the King nodded. "Nothing the likes of this festival has ever been seen, nor will it be again! It is the *perfect* event to transition the kingdom, here, in the presence of all the other kingdoms to signify our bond and strengthen our alliances in such a positive affair." King Hugo nodded, satisfied. "The perfect beginning to Sebastian's reign!"

"Yes, Father, but does the wedding and coronation need to occur so quickly?" Prince Sebastian sat in an elegant, red velvet armchair. He had been sitting perfectly still for almost six hours while the royal artist painted what would be his first royal portrait as King. It would be presented on coronation day.

"No reason to wait, my boy!" the King said heartily. "The sooner it is done, the sooner I can relax!"

"And the sooner you can push my future Queen into having children?"

"I will do nothing of the sort!" the King snapped, before softening. "But surely I will be granted a daughter in law that would not see me go without. *Surely* the right Queen for you, my boy, will be one with a strong maternal instinct." He gazed back out of the window, sighing deeply.

"The right Queen for me will be the right one for the kingdom, Father, you can be assured of that!" Sebastian said.

"Good man!" the Viscount barked.

"This is why the time is right, Son," King Hugo said lovingly. "Your head is in the right place. You will do well, whether the coronation is in ten years or tomorrow."

"It would still have been nice to have more warning, Father. It will be an honour to serve my kingdom and continue all the work you have been doing since the war ended." Sebastian got up out of the chair, stretching tall as he strode over to his father, eliciting an angry yell from the royal artist. "I promise you Father, I will *never* leave this kingdom at risk. It will see growth and prosperity the likes never envisioned before," Sebastian said, holding King Hugo's hands in his own. "And I could not be more humbled that you will be there to see it."

"You are a good man, Sebastian," his father told him. "Not a good painting subject, but a good man, a good son... and you will make an outstanding King. You are strong, responsible, and committed... unlike another son I will not care to name..."

Rufus the acrobat was the very opposite of strong, responsible, and committed, at least in the eyes of those such as the King and the other courtiers. He was throwing juggling batons back and forth with one of the most incredibly talented performers he had ever seen. Her talent had him insatiably jealous, and so he had insisted on taking her up on the challenge to prove he could be just as good.

He was not. The baton fell to the streets with a shattering *clang*, resulting in raucous laughter from the crowd. "Come now, Rufus! You were so sure you could best me!" Bellona called from atop her stilts, still juggling her three remaining batons. "Is that the best you have?"

"Definitely not!" he yelled back. "That is simply the best I can juggle!"

Bellona moved over to the dance platform and slowly sat down so she could remove the stilt legs strapped to her calves. Once released, she threw the bring pink and yellow striped poles over her shoulder and climbed down. "Care to help a lady carry her gear to her quarters?" she asked Rufus.

"Of course!" he answered grandly, looking around. "Do you know any?"

She scoffed, punching him in the arm playfully, as Rufus took the stilts and carried them into a private tent on the far side of the fairgrounds. Once through the entry, Bellona knocked the stilts from his arms and grabbed him by the shirt, dragging Rufus close to her.

Rufus gulped, staring into her dark brown eyes, surrounded by coloured glitter. She moved forward and kissed him deeply. "I... I don't-" he stammered.

"-Shh," Bellona whispered, kissing the side of his face and moving down the left side of his neck. "Surely you are going to let me see you off properly!"

Rufus breathed in sharply as tingles ran down his body, causing his skin to erupt in goosebumps. He closed his eyes as

Bellona kissed her way down his chest, handling his growing member.

He gasped at her touch as she unbuckled his pants, pulling them down as she dropped to her knees. He gasped again as she took him in her mouth, running her tongue back and forth along his organ, which was hardening with every second.

Rufus' head fell back and he reached forward to grip the top of her head, his fingers running through her black, glossy curls. As his grip tightened, so did Bellona's, with her gentle moans providing pleasurable vibrations along his shaft.

Rufus felt his knees begin to go weak. Bellona reached around to his back and gripped his glutes to stabilise him. One of his hands moved down to her shoulder, pulling him back and forth with her movements.

She moved closer, drawing him in deeper. She had completely enveloped him, gripping him even tighter as she moved more and more vigorously. Rufus panted heavily as the blood rushed faster, and when the surge of his body was finally unleashed, Bellona held fast, not releasing him until he was drained of every last drop.

Rufus stumbled backwards as Bellona disengaged from him. She giggled as she eyed him coyly, wiping the corner of her mouth. Rufus bent down to return his pants to their proper place. "Well..." he gulped. "Th-that was quite a goodbye."

"Well I can't have you going and forgetting about me, can I?' she answered, reaching up behind her neck and unclasping the clip of her skin tight performer's outfit, causing the front to fall open, releasing her smooth, round breasts from their binding.

"Then why leave at all?" Rufus asked, tucking his shirt back in. He crossed the room and pulled Bellona into his embrace, kissing her. "Stay with me... You cannot leave."

"Rufus," she whispered, her caramel skin glowing in the afternoon sun. "You know I care for you deeply, but this was all it was ever going to be; all it ever *could* be."

"But it could be more if you stayed?"

"And I cannot," she answered simply. "This is my life. This is my family, and you have yours here also that you must tend to, surely?"

"My family…" Rufus drifted off. "They… they pay very little attention to what I do. They are a very business minded, serious bunch."

"Nothing like you," Bellona said shaking her head, smiling.

"Definitely not," Rufus agreed.

Bellona let the smile drop from her face. "The pack down has begun, Rufus. By the time the sun rises tomorrow, the troupe will be ready to leave… and I will be gone." Rufus made to argue. She placed a finger to his lips. "Your life will continue on… and I will be simply the most pleasant of memories when, one day, you are old and married to the true love of your life, whom you met right here and had the opportunity to truly get to know because she was not a part of a travelling circus act!"

She laughed. Rufus could not help but smile. "That… that *does* sound nice," he told her.

"So go and find her!" she exclaimed, clapping his chest with her hands. "Be gone with you before this becomes the tragic sad goodbye!" she smiled at him. "I would not have that… definitely not." Rufus nodded, and after a final kiss to Bellona's forehead, he exited her tent for the final time.

The summer had lasted much longer than the previous years. As Rufus reminisced over the bittersweet memories of the time he had spent with Bellona, being among the circus folk; it was most freeing. He had spent almost all of his summer days there and many nights besides. He had met so many new and different people from many varied places that he knew most of his family would *never* approve of... except maybe his sister... *especially* when it came to the lithe, strong acrobat women who wore such tight, revealing clothing.

Rufus walked through the streets of the city, relishing his last moments of freedom before he had to return home. He was still covered in the pastel face paints from the circus and while that garnered odd looks, it made it easier to get through the oddly crowded streets as any decent folk made every attempt to avoid such a person.

With the circus having ended the previous night and it being so late in the day, Rufus was rather confused as to why there were so many people on the streets. Everybody seemed in such a hurry and all were talking in highly animated and excited voice.

"I cannot believe it has finally happened!" one women squealed.

"A new King and Queen! Glorious days!"

"Oh to be chosen by the Prince!"

"Excuse me, Miss?" Rufus jumped in front of the women, startling them all. "Did you just say we were getting a new King and Queen? Surely King Hugo is alive and well?"

"Oh!" one of the women gasped, fanning herself at practically being assault by what she saw as a suited clown. "Yes, yes good man, he most certainly is."

"Then why would we be getting a new King and Queen?"

"Haven't you heard, Son?" a man said gruffly from behind him. "There's to be a festival in the coming days! The Prince will choose a wife then they are to be crowned immediately in the days following." He took a deep draw of his pipe, releasing the smoke in small rings. "The King will be abdicating!"

"Never did I think I would see the day!" Rufus exclaimed.

"Nor we," one of the women said. "Good day gentlemen."

"Yes Madam... Good day," he responded softly as they walked quickly on.

Rufus continued down the street, struggling to understand what he had just heard. The *King? Abdicating?* He was so caught up in his thoughts that he did not see the woman in the grey frock half running down the street towards the seamstress, after having informed a general assistant of work that needed doing to a carriage *and* seen to it that a hairstylist would be available for the festival's three days.

He did not see her as he gazed up into the sky and pictured Prince Sebastian and what it would mean to refer to him as *King* Sebastian, just as she was looking down at the remainder of her list for both the meeting and the festival to come. He only saw her, when, due to how little attention either of them were paying to where they were going, they collided.

5

Asche had dashed away from her stepmother and stepsisters the moment they had demanded it, flying so quickly to the kitchen she could have sworn she had wings.

"Argh! Good *Lord* Lass! Wha's chasin' you?" Arina exclaimed, startled by Asche's sudden appearance.

"I need you to tell Gerry that the Contessa wants *gold* embellishments put on the carriage and it *must* be done before the festival," Asche said quickly.

"Wha'? Wha' festival?" she asked.

"*I will explain everything later, I promise!*" she cried, running out the back door. Asche ran as fast as her already swollen feet would allow, back down their street and into the city.

She had stopped in at Madame LeQuoits as quickly as common decency and good manners would allow, then checked in with Greta at the bakery to confirm the order for tomorrow. Asche was almost at the seamstress's shop. Up ahead she could already see a line forming outside of *Oh Sew Elegant!* the city's most highly sought after designer.

Asche looked down at the list she had hastily scribbled on her arm as she ran through the kitchen. She still had to pick up the ribbons to add to the carriage, request a meeting with the Governess that would be ensuring June and Charlotte's mannerisms and royal knowledge were at their peak, collect her father's suit from the tailor and make it home in time to serve dinner and update the Contessa on everything on the list she was given.

So flustered by her list and so focused she was on her tasks that she did not notice when a shadow crossed in front of her and she ran headlong into a painted-faced gentleman as he walked in the opposite direction.

"Mademoiselle!" the man exclaimed. "I am so sorry! Are you alright?"

"Oh!" Asche gasped, almost falling over.

The painted gentleman was able to catch her arm and stop her. He then very quickly released her arm and backed away. "Begging your pardon. Forgive me for handling you in such a manner."

Asche fanned her face with her hand. "N-no it is quite alright. Thank you. I am sor-" she looked up to both her assailant and her saviour. "-Sorry. I... I should have been watching where I was going," she stammered, gazing into his brilliant blue eyes.

The man stared back at her. He held out his hand. "Rufus."

Asche took it and they shook. "Asche. Lovely to meet you."

"Pleasure to meet you, Asche," Rufus said. "You seem to be in a bit of a rush? Preparing for the festival?"

"Oh, yes," Asche answered. "Oh! Yes! I must get to the seamstress!" She turned back to the shop. The line had almost doubled in that short period of time. "Oh no! However will I get the order in now?" she said, distressed.

"You are going to see Madame Fae Marmorante?" Rufus asked.

"Not any longer, it seems," Asche sighed, near tears.

"Here, come with me!" he said, heading down a side street. Asche paused, unsure. "Well? What are you waiting for?"

Asche bit her lip, glancing either way down the main street, before following Rufus. "Where does this lead?"

"Well, this side street has a back alley that leads to the back doors of all the stores along main street," he explained. "And as it so happens-," he said, opening one of the doors with a flourish. "-Madame Fae Marmorante is a friend," he smiled.

Asche felt a rush of gratitude, which was immediately cut off when she crossed the threshold into the back room of the dressmaker's shop. Fabrics of every type, size, colour and pattern hung on giant rolls from floor to ceiling; mannequins with half complete designs created obstacles to move around as they made their way across the space.

"*Nixie!* NIXIE ARE YOU HERE?" Rufus called.

"*Who is that?*" a voice yelled back from the front of the store.

"It is *RUFUS!*"

"WHO?" a round face with a full head of dark brown curls popped into view. "Oh, hello Dear!"

"Yes Madame, it is Rufus! Are you able to see me? I made a bit of a blunder and it has left a dear friend a little lost for hope," he explained.

"Anything for you, Dear!" The body that belonged to the head of curls appeared wearing a sleek royal blue gown and matching sapphire earrings. "I have a line out the door and halfway up the street so I cannot lose too much time, but I will most definitely do what I can!"

"Thank you Madame!" Rufus said graciously, kissing her on the hand. "Nixie, may I present Mademoiselle Asche."

"Greetings Madame Marmorante," Asche bowed low. "Thank you so much for seeing me, and might I say that is such a beautiful dress you are wearing!"

"Why, *thank you* Child!" she answered. "Made by my own hands!"

"The colour is spectacular."

"Peacock blue," she whispered with a wink. "Now, what can I do for you?"

"Oh! I have an order for the Contessa Georgina LaBelle-Baron," she explained. "For her and her daughters-"

"-June and Charlotte?" Madame Marmorante confirmed.

"Yes, Madame."

"Am I correct in presuming they shall want a new gown for each day of the festival?" she asked, a finger to her lips, her eyebrow raised.

"Yes, Madame."

Madame Marmorante nodded. "Yes, yes I think I can get something together in time."

"Oh *thank you* Madame Marmorante!" Asche said, tears springing to her eyes. "Thank you so much!"

She waved away her thanks, enveloping Rufus in a hug. "Anything for this one, Dear. He is a good egg, aren't you Rufus?"

"Why yes, I believe I am!" he laughed as Asche made for the back door. "Thank you for everything Nixie! I shall visit again very soon, I am sure!"

"YOU BETTER!" she yelled, returning to the front of the shop as Rufus joined Asche.

Rufus held the door open for Asche and led her back out into the alley. Asche was amazed at the turn of events. "I cannot thank you enough," she said appreciatively.

"Think nothing of it," Rufus said graciously. "If anything, I was beholden to you for the vicious assault on the street."

Asche laughed. Rufus was wonderfully kind. No one put her at such ease other than Heidi, Arina and Gerry. She loved her father, but she rarely felt comfortable around him. Rufus however made her head light and her heart flutter. His kindness and painted face left her curious, each for different reasons, though she rarely experienced either, and never at the same time.

"I believe I most definitely will be thinking about it... for a very long time," she said to him boldly.

He smiled. "Well, I am glad for that. I would rather you not forget me," he said. "Say Asche, will you be attending the King's festival?"

"Oh, I certainly hope so!" Asche answered. "It... it will depend on my-my parents, of course."

"Surely they would see to it that you attend? The chance to become Queen? What parents would withhold you from such an opportunity?"

"I have duties at home," she said honestly. "I do hope with all my heart to attend... though maybe not for reason of the Prince..." Asche glanced at him. "I will do my best to be there."

"Then I shall wait for you each day until you arrive!" Rufus announced.

Asche's smile grew. "I must get home," she said. "I have much to do. Besides the King's festival, my family has an event we are hosting tomorrow."

"Then I shall not take up any of your time," he nodded formally. He took her hand, placing on it a gentle kiss, just a brush of the lips. Asche felt a tingle run up her arm from where he kissed. He withdrew "Oh, before I forget, Madame Marmorante gave me these." From his jacket Rufus pulled out two tight coils of gold ribbon.

Asche gasped. "How did she know?" She reached out and took the ribbon. "They are for the carriage."

"Oh, Nixie is magical like that; forever intuitive to her customer's needs," Rufus said. "Or maybe a messenger was sent ahead of you?"

"Perhaps," she said curiously.

"Farewell Asche," Rufus said, bowing grandly. "It has been positively delightful meeting you today. Until we meet again." He then tipped his hat and headed towards the city centre.

Asche turned in the opposite direction, in a daze as she made her final stops at the tailor, who, luckily, was open later than usual due to the King's announcement, and the Governess Theresa's, who declared that it would be the greatest of pleasures to whip the young ladies of the LaBelle-Baron household into shape for the festival and that she would be at the mansion at eight o'clock sharp for their morning session.

With Rufus having rescued her afternoon, Asche made her way slowly home, appreciating the ability to dawdle after having spent the day exhausting herself running from one side of the city to the other. Once again, she entered their property from the back gate, stopping at the towering hazel tree by the fence. She was pleased to have the luxury of time to sit for moment by the tree. It was rare she had the opportunity to do so.

"Hello Mother," she whispered. "I have had the most intriguing day." She proceeded to tell the tree about the festival and the gowns and Madame Marmorante... and Rufus.

The tree held great value to Asche, for her Mother was buried beside it, or rather, the tree had been planted next to the grave. Digby Baron used to travel quite a lot after Asche's mother, Victoria had died, especially in the early days of his marriage to Contessa Georgina. June and Charlotte would ask for dresses, toys, the latest trinkets and jewellery; Asche would ask for his safe return or a simple pressed leaf, flower or feather. She would keep them in a journal as a memoir of his travels, taking rubbings with a charcoal pencil.

On one specific trip, Asche's father had delivered her a beautiful bluebird feather and she noticed a twig stuck in his hat. "Father! Do groom yourself properly!" she had laughed, earning herself a scowl and a scold from her stepmother.

Asche had taken the twig and planted it in the dirt by her mother's headstone. She would sit by the twig and sing, or cry, depending on her mood and the events of that day. Over time it had grown into the towering hazel tree before her now.

Digby had been amazed at the tree's rapid growth, commenting on it only to Asche where Georgina could not hear. The Contessa was simply thrilled she could no longer see the grave due to the wide, twisting branches.

Asche stayed on the stone bench by the tree for as long as she could, only getting up when the sun's rays touched the uppermost branches.

6

The next day was hectic for the LaBelle-Baron household. The Governess Theresa arrived on their doorstep at eight o'clock sharp, exactly as promised. June and Charlotte required much prompting to get out of bed and dressed in time.

Much like the day before Asche was sent running into town, first to collect the bakery order for the Charity Women's League meeting that was to be held from promptly twelve noon but also to collect the first of the festival gowns for the following day.

Both June and Charlotte had begun squealing madly when she returned with them, but Georgina quickly took them from her hands and disappeared all three. "Ladies!" she admonished. "The Women's Charity League will be here any minute. There isn't the *time* to see or try on the dresses now! You will have to wait for this afternoon!"

They grumbled and pouted but went about preparing themselves to receive guests. "You, Cinderella, are to remain in your room. Am I clear?" the Contessa commanded.

Asche let her head drop. "Yes, Stepmother." This occurred whenever the household held an event. Asche would be sent to her room where she would not be seen and her father would speak of her as though she were away at a fancy boarding school and the Contessa would not speak of her at all as though she had died when her mother did.

Asche made to climb the stairs to the second storey, where she would walk to the end of the hallway to the door that led to her little attic bedroom. As she reached the first step, she stopped. "Stepmother?" she began tentatively, turning back to Contessa. Georgina raised an eyebrow in response. "I was wondering if I-well, if I could attend the King's festival?" Her stepmother's eyebrows shot into her hair. Asche hurried on before she could lose her nerve. "I promise that I would be on my best behaviour, and I needn't have a fancy gown, and of *course* I have no interest in seeking out the Prince and... and the decree *did say* that all maidens are invited to attend," she finished flatly, looking at the tiles under her feet.

Contessa Georgina remained silent for an incredibly long time. Asche slowly looked up, thinking that perhaps she had walked away entirely, but there she stood. "I... shall consider it," she answered finally.

"Oh, thank you Stepmother!" Asche said quickly, before turning on her heels and running up the stairs before Georgina could say anything more.

One in her room, Asche closed and bolted her door, immediately moving to the window where the palace could be seen clearly in the distance. There was a noise below her. She glanced down from her window and saw the first carriage pull into the driveway, carrying the first attendee of the House of LaBelle-Baron's Women's Charity League meeting.

Asche sighed happily, then giggled, before letting herself fall backwards onto the bed. Rufus was quite handsome. At least, she *thought* he was based on what she could see under the face paint. Was it possible she would be able to spend the next three days with him, exploring the palace grounds, laughing and eating? Dancing to the musicians? It seemed like a child's fantasy, but there it was, almost within her reach. She was determined to make sure she attended. She would prove to the Contessa that she deserved to go.

She continued to think of Rufus throughout the day and when the heat of the attic became too much, she pulled off her dress as well as her underclothes, discarding it all over a chair. "Much better," she sighed.

She ran her finger along her thigh, her eyes closed, and continued to think of Rufus, blushing ever so slightly as her fingers began to drift.

♠

Prince Sebastian Reginald Hubert Matthew Bishop the Seventh was pacing his quarters. He had spent most of his day being fitted for as many suits as he had names. He required a different one for each day of the festival, one for the wedding, one for his father's abdication ceremony and one for his coronation.

"Come now, Brother!" his younger brother Vladimir was saying as he sat on the chaise at the foot of his colossal four poster bed. "Surely getting married cannot be as fearful as you are making it out to be!"

"I am not *scared* Vlad, I am simply annoyed that the choice was not mine!"

"But it *will* be yours!" Vladimir insisted enthusiastically. "You will have your pick of every unmarried woman in *every* kingdom in the land! They will all be right here. You will find one that sparks your fire, just you wait and see! The kingdom's next Queen will be everything you desire, I am sure of it!"

"You are an optimist and a fool, Brother," Sebastian said to Vladimir jokingly.

"Better a foolish optimist than a dreary academic drowning in loneline-!"

"–Talking about me again, are we?" Zarina strode into the room and a sweeping gown of green velvet, a mile long train following her. "I *told* you I am not lonely at all, I simply prefer being alone to surrounding myself with sycophants and yes men."

"Entertaining as watching you become defensive is, Sister," Vladimir said. "It is not you we were referring to."

"Oh?" Zarina said. "Well, that's a change. Then I presume it is *your* marriage you are discussing, Sebastian?"

"Unfortunately so."

"Yes, it must be *terrible* to have your life dictated by the expectations of others, marrying whoever you are told whenever you are told," Zarina sighed dramatically. "I could not *possibly* relate." She crossed her arms and winked at Vladimir.

Sebastian scoffed. "Yes, Zarina, and you are now benefitting off my forced marriage by writing the terms for your own! How is that fair?"

"How is it fair that, as a woman, I am able to choose when I marry?"

"That is not what I meant and you know it!" Sebastian yelled. "By saying you would marry when I was King you forced father's hand! Now he gets two for one! Two marriages and likely two grandchildren within the year! Except *your* marriage is one you choose for yourself *when* you choose!"

"I have a time limit too, Sebastian. All your coronation does is buy me a little more, and you are talking as though you have no choices? Surely having access to any woman across the *fourteen* kingdoms is enough to find yourself someone you can see a future with?" Zarina asked. "Unless you are simply going to spend the next three days fulfilling every hedonistic desire you have with as many of them as will have you, utterly ignoring the future entirely until Father finally forces you to make a decision and *you will not have one?*" Zarina tilted her head questioningly; knowingly. "Then who do you think he is going to ask who the Queen should be?"

Sebastian frowned. He hated that his sister knew him so well. "If that happens-"

"-*When* that happens," Zarina said, eyebrow raised.

"*If* that happens," Sebastian said again. "Who would it be? Who would you have be the Queen?"

Zarina had not one second's hesitation. "The Princess of Nowhorl," she sighed. "Willow. She is *perfect*; intelligent, eloquent, well read, diplomatic, kind; she is a woman of the people and her people *love* her."

"And our people?" Vladimir asked.

"Well, that is the thing, isn't it?" Zarina said excitedly. She often became this way when talking politics. It was one of the things the Viscount insisted had prevented Zarina from finding a suitable match before now. "Our kingdoms are the largest of the fourteen and while we are most certainly *friendly* with Nowhorl, we have no trade ties or other binding agreements. A marriage solidifying the bond between our nations would guarantee peace and prosperity for *generations!*"

"Are you asking me to consider her, Zarina?" Sebastian asked. "I thought this was supposed to be *my* choice?"

"And it is!" she answered. "And no, I am not. Princess Willow is most certainly the best candidate, however you did not ask who I thought you should *choose,* you asked who I thought should be *Queen.*"

"Is that not the same thing?" Vladimir laughed uncertainly, confusion on his face.

"No," Zarina said simply, before making for the door, waving. "Good afternoon gentlemen!" The door slammed shut behind her.

"You know, Brother?" Sebastian said. "I *am* going to do what is best for our kingdom."

"I know you will Sebastian. You will amaze us all, I am sure," Vladimir nodded.

"No, I mean it! When I am King, Father is going to see just what I am willing to do and what lengths I am willing to travel to see our kingdom happy, healthy, thriving and *protected!*" Sebastian began to rant feverishly. "I am going to make sure there are so many new babies he will not be able to play with them all, there will be so much protection at our borders no one will ever dare threaten us and our people are going to have *everything* they deserve!"

"*Alright* Brother, alright!" Vladimir laughed. "I believe you!"

"I am going to start... with Nowhorl."

"Well, securing a bride to be Queen, anyhow."

"Yes..." Sebastian whispered. "First the bride... then Nowhorl."

7

O n the other side of the city, Asche was pulling at the cord of the corseted backs of June and Charlotte's dresses. June's dress for the first day was a blood orange. It had a large bustle at the back and simple layering at the front. The embroidered sleeves came down to her elbows and the same pattern covered the bodice to the waist.

Charlotte was wearing a dusty pink dress that went all the way up to her neck and full length sleeves. While more reserved than her sister, Asche thought she looked quite lovely.

"Cinderella, I *do* hope you bathed before handling the dresses!" June was complaining. "Your hands feel rather sweaty."

"Well, I certainly bathed once I had returned from collecting the dresses, June," Asche answered. "But the attic is rather warm so I am quite sweaty, I suppose," she grunted, pulling the final section of the cord tight and tying it off.

"Oh, are the quarters you have been provided so lovingly not to your liking, Cinderella?" the Contessa's cold voice interrupted. She slinked into the room, wearing a body fitting black gown that flared out dramatically at the knees. It had a large, elevated neckline and a massive satin rose sewn onto the hip.

"No!" Asche gasped, releasing June's corset and stepping back. She placed her hands behind her back and lowered her head. "I am most thankful for what I have, Stepmother."

"It certainly does not seem like it," Georgina snapped, opening her black feathered fan. "You would expect to join us at the King's *festival* where my daughters are to meet the *Prince* while you stand here before us spitting on all we have given you? What a charade that would be?"

"I am so sorry, Stepmother," Asche said. "Please forgive me. I never meant to offend!"

"No... of course not," Georgina sneered. "See that it does not happen again, or you may just have to see if the *barn* is more sufficient for your needs than the attic," she threatened.

Asche held back the tears as she moved onto Charlotte's dress. She carefully pulled together the light floaty material, taking a deep breath with every button she did up as she forced herself into a false calm. The last thing she had wanted to do was offend her stepmother and stepsisters; all she had ever wanted was for them to love and accept her as their family. Now, she had quite possibly ruined her chance.

She made a resolution; she was going to ensure Georgina and her stepsisters never doubted her love and commitment to them ever again. She would work doubly hard and do twice much, never accepting help from Heidi and Arina again if necessary. She *would* do right by her family; she *would* show them that she loved and respected them, and she *would* go to the King's festival.

The sun rose on the morning of the first day of the festival. Asche's heart leapt as the sun's rays woke her from her sleep. Her feet followed. She raced from her attic bedroom to the kitchen basement, finding Arina had already started breakfast.

"There you are!" she exclaimed. "I was wonderin' wha' was keepin' you!"

"I am sorry I overslept!" Asche huffed. "Let me help!"

"I'm havin' i' on, Lass! Heidi and I specifically le' you sleep so you'd be ready for the big day!" Arina said excitedly.

Asche ran to the maid and hugged her fiercely. "I love you, Arina."

"We love you too, darlin'," she said softly, hugging her back. "Now, you go an' sor' a dress!"

Asche gasped. "Of course! I have just the thing!" She got onto her tiptoes and gave Arina a kiss on her forehead. Then she ran all the way back to her room and opened her wardrobe, pulling out an old apple green dress with wide, puffy sleeves. She spent the morning picking apart the sleeves until they fell loose and repairing the inner lining. She also added embellishments to the bodice and ribbons around the waist.

She continued working until she heard the tell tale call of "CINDERELLA!" from downstairs.

"Yes June? Charlotte?" Asche said as she entered their room.

"Where have you *been* all morning?" June asked furiously. "Help me!" Asche helped her into her net and corset, then laced up the back of her gown before starting with Charlotte's buttons.

"I am sorry," Asche said as the dress slowly took shape on Charlotte's body. "I was making preparations for... for the festival," she finished lamely.

"Is the carriage ready?" Charlotte asked.

"I imagine it would be. Gerry has been working on it for two days," Asche answered. "Shall I run down and confirm?" She finalised the last of Charlotte's buttons.

"Yes, do," June said. "You *must* be downstairs for when Madame LeQuoits and Governess Theresa arrive to see them in *immediately!* And see to it that there is a tea tray ready when they do!"

"Yes June," Asche nodded, making for the door. She stopped short when she saw Contessa Georgina standing in the doorway. "Good morning Stepmother," she said quietly. "I was just going to see to the carriage and the tea tray for Madame LeQuoits and Governess Theresa."

Georgina stared at her, her mouth a hard line, then she stepped into the room, leaving the doorway clear. Asche stepped quickly through it, then took the time to take a breath before she ran to the kitchen.

"Do we have a tea tray handy?" she asked Heidi, who was packing away the last of the breakfast things.

Heidi was a short, older woman, with wispy greying hair and light green eyes. Her arms were long and thin, and moved as though she were floating. She insisted it was a call back to her finishing school days. "Naturally!" she answered brightly.

"Can you boil the water for me please, Heidi? I have to prepare it for Madame LeQuoits and Governess Theresa."

"I shall see to it, Love-"

"-Thank you so much! Have you seen Gerry?"

"He's out with the carriage; just putting on the final touches."

"Perfect! I shall-"

"-Shall *what* Cinderella?" a cold voice interrupted. "What shall you do while Heidi and I do *your* job in greeting our guests and serving them tea?"

"I-I... Well, with the tea being seen to, I was going to... I did not realise Madame LeQuoits and Governess Theresa had *arrived* yet," Asche stammered.

"Indeed, they have," Georgina said icily. "Heidi, the tray, if you please?"

"Yes, Mistress," Heidi said, bustling past her with the tray and disappearing up the stairs.

"Well, Cinderella?" Georgina asked again. "What was so important that you were pushing your duties onto other hard-working people?"

"I was seeing to it that *all* the preparations were ready, Stepmother. It required me to be in many places. Heidi was simply helping me," Asche tried to explain. The Contessa continued to glare. Asche lowered her head. "I... I was seeing to my dress... for the festival," she finally admitted.

"Oh so you will disregard your duties to see that you are prepared to attend the King's festival, and by so doing fail to complete the necessary requirements to attend in the first place!" she hissed poisonously. "Once again you prove your lack of respect for or dedication to the very family you insist you wish to attend with!"

"That is not true!" Asche said desperately. "I *am* dedicated to this family! I promise you Stepmother! How can I prove it?"

The Contessa Georgina regarded her calmly. Then, "You wish to prove it, Cinderella?" she asked as she crossed the kitchen, to the dry store.

"Very much, Stepmother," Asche said insistently.

She collected a pot of lentils that had been sitting drying out on one of the shelves and carried them to the fireplace. "You wish to attend the festival? You wish to prove your love for your family?" She dumped the lentils into the ashes of the fireplace. "Then you will dig every single lentil from the fireplace and return them to the pot," she declared, letting the pot fall to the floor with an almighty *crash*.

Asche threw herself to floor by the fireplace the moment she heard the door slam closed. She worked for what felt like hours, carefully sifting through all of the ash and soot in the fireplace, removing the lentils as she found them, placing them back into the pot at her side. Her fingers became blacker as she worked, and it steadily travelled up her hands and covered her legs and lap.

Asche worked diligently, not allowing a single lentil to be left behind, not letting any slip by her sight. Her eyes began to ache and water, but she did not risk wiping them lest she got soot in her eyes. Then where would she be?

Her back and arms felt stiff and sore when she finally sat back on her heels and surveyed the once again full pot. She would have started crying from the relief if she had the time to do so, but she could hear Gerry outside readying the horses. She had to get ready.

She came across the Contessa, June and Charlotte in the foyer as she reached the stairs. Their hair and makeup had been fully done. Asche would not have time for such finery, but then, she did not feel as though she needed it given the Prince was not her goal. "Stepmother! I have done it!" she said happily. "Every single lentil!"

Contessa Georgina's face was inscrutable. She looked Asche from top to toe, before sighing and shaking her head. "Well you certainly can*not* join us like that! We will be meeting your father in the entrance hall and he would be positively *horrified* to see you in that state!"

Asche laughed. "No! Definitely not!" She looked down at the torn, dirty gown. "I shall bathe and change immediately. I promise I shan't keep you waiting!"

"See to it that you do not!" Georgina yelled back as Asche made for the stairs. "We go to the carriage!"

"Mother!" she heard June cry out as she reached the second floor landing. "You *cannot* be serious!"

She ignored the argument, too excited to be concerned about June's anger, until she suddenly heard the anger change to glee, as raucous laughter followed her to her bedroom. Asche crossed the threshold and froze, as she saw her once beautiful dress hanging in tatters on the mannequin.

A sound of the horses neighing brought Asche back to her body, the shock wearing off just in time to see the carriage trundle down the driveway and towards the palace without her.

Asche stared out the window for a second more, before running back down the three flights of stairs, out the kitchen door and across the yard to the hazel tree. There she remained as her heart broke and sore body ached, weeping every tear her body held within her.

She thought she might stay there forever, just waiting until her body was finally absorbed into her mother's tombstone and she became one with the hazel tree. What wakened her from her grief was a bright light flashing on the other side of her closed eyelids. She opened them, curiosity getting the better of her. In front of her floated a golden dust mote, just the tiniest speck.

As Asche watched it, it began to grow, getting bigger and bigger until she had to close her eyes again, shielding her face with her hand. When the light died down, she peeked through her fingers.

"Impossible!" she gasped.

8

ufus waited anxiously at the entrance to the palace. Despite being a festival for Prince Sebastian to select a Queen and therefore having every maiden in the land invited to attend, gentleman of the kingdom's households had been invited also; at Prince Sebastian's request himself.

Why? Because many women would be rather put out at not having been chosen, and to have the eligible men also in attendance to court the poor, heartbroken young ladies would see many suitable matches throughout the kingdom. It was a multi staged plan.

First, many young women from neighbouring kingdom's would immigrate to marry the fine gentlemen here, creating the primary population boom. Then those marriages would result in the birth of *many* children, creating a secondary population boom that would see immense growth and prosperity for the kingdom.

Rufus thought the plan quite ingenious when he thought about it. Invite ladies from other kingdoms to marry the men from this one! King Hugo received the grandchildren that the kingdom was all too aware he longed for, while Prince Sebastian's reign was brought in with a year of monumental growth for the kingdom that would see his transition to power as a positive one for the entire nation. It was a win-win-win all round for the royal family and the soon-to-be King.

Rufus was simply thrilled to have his duties ceased long enough to attend... and have the opportunity to see Asche again. He awaited her eagerly, watching every maiden that passed through the grand archway, examining every face for hers. Every dress was so brightly coloured, as though a parade of parrots were entering the palace, each carriage in a different size, shape and colour; it was like watching a bunch of giant jewelled insects crawl up the drive.

There were many beautiful ladies entering; many fine gentlemen also, but none of them were Asche.

♠

Down in the carriage line, where fifty footmen were seeing to every carriage arriving for the first day of the festival, Contessa Georgina had arrived with her daughters. June and Charlotte were delicately led down the stairs and onto the main walk that led through the gardens and up the main palace steps.

"Hold your heads high Ladies!" Georgina called behind her as she climbed the stairs.

"Why do there have to be so many stairs?" Charlotte complained, fanning herself with the hand that wasn't busy holding up her skirts.

"Hush, Charlotte!" June snapped. "My dress is *twice* the weight of yours and I can manage!"

"You spend far more time in heavy dresses such as these," Charlotte grumbled.

"Thus *showing*," their mother put in purposefully. "*Just* how much you could learn by following June's example!"

The three women reached the top of the stairs, where they were greeted by the sweeping bows of the ushers. "Fair morning, Ladies!" one of them greeted.

"Fair morning to you too, Sir," Georgina greeted him lightly. "The Contessa LaBelle and her daughters. Has my husband, the Conte Baron, arrived, perchance?"

The usher checked his list of names on a long yellow scroll with several red wax seals. "Yes, Contessa, he has indeed checked in. Escorts are waiting at the entrance to the banquet hall," he explained.

"Maidens will be announced every night at the evening ball, thereby ensuring the Prince is personally introduced to each lady. "June and Charlotte LaBelle of the Baron household... are to be introduced on the second night," he informed them.

"Oh my daughters *must* be introduced tonight! They must be the *first* faces Prince Sebastian sees!" Contessa Georgina insisted.

"I am sorry Madame, but I hold no sway over the introductions," the usher explained. "I simply have the list to inform the guests appropriately."

"What is your name?"

"S-Simon, Madame."

"Surely, *Simon*," Georgina said softly, moving very close the usher's ear, running her gloved finger down the buttoned front of his shirt. "There is *something* you could do?"

Simon gulped and cleared his throat. "I... I will see what I can do."

A smile slowly crept onto Georgina's face. "I would most definitely have to repay you if you did." She grasped his shoulder tightly before the women continued on through the wide entryway into the banquet hall.

At the open doorway to the banquet hall, Digby Baron was waiting in his best red and black double breasted suit with shiny black shoes. When his wife entered, she smiled graciously as he gave her a gentle kiss on the cheek. "Ah, Georgina, radiant as ever!" he said warmly. "June, Charlotte, you look beautiful."

"Thank you!" they chorused.

"Where is Asche?" he asked.

"Taken ill-"

"-Decided against it-"

"-Said she had a pressing task to attend to-"

"-She may be along later, however," Contessa Georgina said, taking her husband's arm. "Arina is taking good care of her! And the festival lasts three days after all. Come, Digby, let us see what delectable morsels the palace has provided."

Digby gazed back through the entryway, as though expecting Asche to suddenly appear. He looked back to his wife, who eyed him expectantly. "Y-yes, of course, Dear. Let us go."

While the men in her life were wondering where she was, Asche was staring in awe at the apparition in from of her. In a glowing silver dress with a matching hooded robe and shining brown hair piled high on her head, was a woman with smooth, dark skin carrying a long golden wand.

"Hello, Child," the woman greeted her kindly, as though they had known each other many years. "It saddens me to see you so unhappy, my dear."

"Wh-who are you?" Asche stammered, her eyes wide as she stared.

"I? Why, I am your Fairy Godmother," she smiled. "Do you not know me?"

Asche looked closer, gazing into the woman's eyes. She gasped in recognition. "Madame Marmorante!"

"*Nixie!* Hello Darling," she said. "Whatever brings you to such sadness?"

"I..." Asche's eyes welled up from the memories of the destroyed dress and her stepmother and stepsisters evil laughter. "I thought I was to attend the King's festival."

"And why don't you?" Nixie asked flatly, as though the solution to Asche's problem was rather obvious.

"Well the carriage is gone and my dress was destroyed... and I am *awfully* dirty," Asche explained.

"Oh pish!" Nixie said dismissively, waving her arm. "Surface problems *entirely*. We must start with the carriage! *Follow me!*"

She strode off through the back of the property with a purposeful gait, so much so that Asche struggled to keep up. "Where are we going?" she called out to the seamstress.

"To the vegetable patch, of *course!*" she answered.

"H-how do you know we *have* a vegetable patch?"

Madame Fae Marmorante turned on the spot mid stride, almost causing Asche to run headlong into her. Luckily, she pulled herself up short before the collision. "I know everything, my dear. I was your mother's Fairy Godmother also. I have followed your entire family for almost 600 years; keeping them safe, offering them guidance; now I watch over you. I have been here all your life, Asche. Who do you think guided the hazel twig into the perfect place in the soil by your mother's grave? Provided the love, light and warmth needed for it to sprout? What else could explain its growth... but *magic?*"

Asche looked back at the hazel tree, tears of a different kind making her eyes sting. "Were... were you there when-"

"-It was I who carried her, my dear," Nixie said softly, placing a cool hand on her cheek. "I took her pain away in her final moments and led into the after."

Asche turned back to her, almost angrily, which disappeared the moment she saw that Nixie also had tears welling in her eyes. "Is she alright? In... the after?"

"It is a place of peace and happiness, Child. A place she well deserves," Nixie said, just fanning her eyes and blinking away the tears. She pointed the golden wand at Asche almost aggressively. "Just as *you* deserve to be at that festival!"

She turned back around and continued on to the vegetable patch, where she pointed her wand at the largest pumpkin. It shot out of the patch, bounced off a tree and landed with a *thwump* in the grass. Then, before Asche's very eyes, it began to grow. She stared, her mouth hanging open in shock, as the orange hue of the giant squash turned yellow, then white, then silver, as it grew into a large round carriage, complete with curly vined wheels.

"Next, something must *pull* the carriages!" Nixie said in a business-like fashion. She looked around the garden and found a group of mice sitting on an exposed tree root, chewing away at a stolen zucchini. "Ah! *You!*" She waved her wand.

"Oh please do not hurt them!" Asche cried. Her voice died as she watched the tiny bodies expand just as the pumpkin had and within a full minute Asche was no longer looking a field mice, but four white chargers. "Wow!"

"What's next?" Nixie asked, bustling about the garden.

"There is *more?*" Asche asked incredulously.

"Of *course* my darling!" Nixie said indignantly. "You cannot attend the festival without an escort! And of course someone needs to *drive* the carriage." She continued to look around the garden, before catching her eye on two bright green lizards by the fountain. "You shall do nicely!"

Another wave of her wand turned the small green lizards into lithe little men in smart footmen attire, with yet another catching a large toad that was sitting on a rock in the fountain. It gave a startled *croak* as it began to swell, its limbs lengthening and its bulbous body stretching out into the torso of a tall man with a large navy top hat to match his coachman's suit.

Asche continued to gape. "This isn't possible!"

"And yet it is!" Madame Fae-Nixie sighed. "Go on, off you go!"

Nixie began to shoo her into the carriage. "But-but I cannot possibly go-!"

"-Of *course* you can, Dear!" Nixie interrupted. "Do not let your stepmother deny you a life of happiness simply because she feels none herself!"

"That is not what I mean to say," Asche tried to explain. "I mean... I cannot possibly go like *this*." She indicated her tattered dress and soot covered body.

"Oh! Definitely *not!*" she exclaimed. She waved her wand above Asche's head and a cold tingling began in the roots of her hair, travelling down her body to the tips of her toes.

She kept her eyes closed, anxious for the strange sensation to be over. When the tingling dissipated, she opened her eyes. Her hands and fingers were clean and manicured, and on the other side of them were the beautiful royal blue skirts that struck a familiar chord within Asche. "It is the dress you were wearing at the shop!" she gasped.

"With some minor changes," Nixie winked, waving her wand again. A massive gilded mirror appeared hovering in the air in front of Asche. She was right. The high collar had been lowered and the bustle had been removed. Unlike her stepsisters there was no cage underneath, allowing the skirts to flow freely. The bodice of the dress, all the way to the ends of the long sleeves were covered in lace of the same royal blue colour.

"It is wonderful," Asche whispered. "How can I ever repay you?"

"You can go and find Rufus at that festival and have an *excellent* time!" she laughed, smacking her on the bottom through the dress. "Now! Into the carriage!"

Asche giggled, running towards it. She stopped as her feet hit the grass; her bare feet. "Oh."

"What is it, Dear?"

"I have no shoes..." he said softly.

"Ah! Not to worry Dear! I have *just* the thing!" And with a wave of her wand, her feet were covered with the most beautiful pair of slippers Asche had ever seen.

"Are they-?"

"-*Silver!*" Nixie trilled excitedly. "They are *perfect!* Ties the whole outfit together, don't you think?"

Asche nodded, overwhelmed. She climbed into the carriage with the assistance of lizard-man number one and took a seat on the soft, cushioned seat. "Thank you for everything," she said emotionally.

"Do not thank me yet!" Nixie said. "Beware! The magic shall only last until midnight of the final day of the festival. At the final stroke of the hour, all will be as it was."

"Midnight..." Asche repeated in a hushed whisper. "I will not forget! Thank you again!"

"Think nothing of it, my dear," she answered, then she continued to wave as the toad coachman gave the reins a shake and led the pumpkin carriage down the drive, led by the mice horses. The Fairy Godmother continued to wave until the carriage had disappeared completely. "Cinderella *indeed*," she chuckled to herself, before disappearing in a flash of light.

9

Asche felt more and more nervous the closer she came to the palace, her excitement growing with every passing minute. When the carriage turned into the wide street that led to the giant palace gates, Asche began fanning her skirts in an attempt to cool herself down. Between the anxiousness her actions were causing and the sweltering summer, she was beginning to sweat. She did not want to find Rufus only to have her Fairy Godmother's work gone to waste by arriving in such a state.

When the carriage came to a standstill and her footmen opened the door with a gracious bow, Asche quickly stopped performing the unladylike motions and stepped down from the once-pumpkin as delicately as she could, fearful of ruining the silver slippers.

The festival had long since started. This suited Asche just fine, for it meant being able to slip in unnoticed. She made her way up the stairs and through the entryway, stopping at the large open courtyard that acted as a banquet hall.

Asche was amazed. Long wooden tables of solid oak, lacquered to give them a gorgeous sheen surrounded the hall. On each were trays of food of every kind; cakes, meats, pastries, cheeses and fruits; Asche had never seen so much all in one place. She carefully made her way down the stairs to zero fanfare, something she much appreciated.

At the first table she selected a strawberry. The only strawberries she had been able to have since her mother died were those that had started to turn whilst in the patch. The best one always went directly to the Contessa, and occasionally to her stepsisters if they did not take the fancy of the Contessa that day. Asche took a second, then a third, before finally walking away from the table to see what else the banquet had to offer.

She grew concerned that her stepmother might find her before she found Rufus, until a quiet voice whispered behind her, "What are you *doing* here?"

"Charlotte!" Asche gasped.

"Where did you get that dress?"

"I-it was given to me," Asche stammered. "You won't tell the Contessa, will you?"

Charlotte gaped at her, still coming out of her shock. "Can you imagine her reaction when she is told? *I* certainly won't be the one to place her in such a state!"

Asche exhaled with relief. "Thank you, Charlotte. I promise. I am here to see a friend, then I shall return home. I will not interfere with June or the Prince or... or anything else!"

Charlotte looked scared. "If Mother or June see you... Though I shall be surprised if they *recognise* you!"

"I will maintain my distance. I shall... go and explore the gardens!" Asche nodded resolutely. "I cannot cause any trouble there!" And before Charlotte could respond, Asche turned down a row of tables laden with tall, many layered platters, piled high with delicately iced cakes. She took one, then another, and another as she passed, heading for the tall hedges of the garden she could see through the archway in front of her.

Once on the other side, she breathed a sigh of relief and took a bite of one of the cakes. It was one of the most delicious things she had ever tasted. The closest she had ever come to such delectable flavour since her childhood were the scraps she was able to find from Greta's cakes during the clean up after the Women's Charity League meetings.

Asche made her way through the gardens, revelling in the beauty of the summer blooms. The scent of the roses reminded her of home, but of course their roses were nowhere near the size of these ones, and they only had yellow roses. Here at the palace were roses of every single colour. It was like standing within a rainbow.

Asche paused. *What was that noise?* She moved towards it. She came around a corner in the hedge just as a giggle came from around the next bend. Asche turned again and gasped, a slight squeal escaping her lips.

A woman with silky smooth, chocolate skin with long dark curls had her head thrown back, the front buttons of her golden yellow gown undone exposing a pair of large, round breasts. Another woman with the darkest red hair fondled them both as she kissed her way along them and up the woman in yellow's collarbone to her neck.

Asche stood stock still, unable to move, staring as the women gripped each other tightly, moaning loudly. Asche began to feel flushed, as her thighs grew moist and the heat rose to her face. She could see that the yellow dress had been pulled up to the dark woman's thigh, while the redhead now had one of her hands up within the folds, causing the woman in yellow to moan louder.

Only when a series of loud trumpets began back in the palace, did the three women come back to their senses. The redhead looked up. "The ball is starting!" She jumped up, turning just in time to see Asche flee.

♠

On the other side of the palace, in a deserted corridor, a palace usher was panting heavily, as he drove his hardened shaft deep into the wet and welcoming folds into a woman with curled raven locks. She was pressed up against the wall, panting heavily as his thrusts became harder and harder.

The usher reached around her body, groping at her breasts, grasping at her throat, as he began to lose himself inside her. He moves his hands back around, ripping her skirts up higher so he could reach her bare cheeks. He held them, one in each hand, spreading them wide to allow him to slam into her as hard as he was able, finally releasing himself and eliciting a loud crying moan from her.

They remained where they were, panting heavily, he struggling to remain upright as his body drained, she feeling her thighs slick with him. "So," the woman finally managed to say. "I believe we have a bargain?"

"Yes, Madame," Simon the usher puffed. "Your daughters will be the first announced tonight." The Contessa Georgina grinned evilly.

♠

Prince Sebastian and Prince Vladimir stood at the balcony overlooking the ballroom. "Well, Son?" King Hugo began. "Are you ready?"

"I do not think I shall ever be *ready* Father," Sebastian answered. "But I am prepared to do whatever is necessary to do right by your kingdom."

"I would expect nothing less," he answered.

"Oh, you two are so *serious* about everything!" Vladimir insisted. "Father, we have trained all our lives, and as you say, you are *abdicating* not dying! You will be here a long time yet, offering your guidance and wisdom," he said.

"He is right Father," Sebastian said. "The kingdom shall have the privilege of having *two* Kings overseeing its happiness!"

King Hugo *harrumphed*, but he still smiled beneath his moustache and beard. "Ah, here we are!" he said as the trumpets began. "Let us see what the other kingdoms have to offer, eh?"

"MAY I PRESENT TO YOU, YOUR GREAT MAJESTY KING HUGO CUTHBERT PHILLIPE BARTHOLOMEW FREDERIC BISHOP THE FOURTH!" The announcer waved his arm, directing the attention of the guests to the King, who clapped loudly.

"Good evening, esteemed guests!" King Hugo called. "It is my great pleasure to welcome you all to very first *Royal Festival!*" More clapping. The King bowed his head graciously. "I have the great honour and privilege of welcoming you all to be a part of this momentous occasion!"

"Tonight is to be the first night of the festival balls, and in two day's time, at the final ball and indeed, the final *event* of the festival, my son and heir, *Prince Sebastian Reginald Hubert Matthew Bishop the Seventh*, your future *King* will select... a *bride!*"

There were claps and cheers as the crowd's energy rose. "LET US MEET THE FIRST OF THESE CANDIDATES, SHALL WE? USHERS! *If you please?*" A hushed silence fell over the crowd as the King backed away from the edge of the balcony and took a seat on the throne.

"Hello! Forgive my lateness!" Zarina whispered, sliding into place on Sebastian's right, just as Vladimir stood to his left.

"You are just in time, Sister," Vladimir said, watching Sebastian attentively. "Just in time to see Sebastian faint with fear!"

"Hush, Vlad," Zarina frowned. "Leave him be. You will be *fine* Sebastian! Just let your heart guide your actions and do not pressure yourself to make a selection until you have met them all. You never know who you could make a connection with!" she said.

Sebastian nodded, anxious. He left his father, brother and sister, walking down the stairs to join the usher who would be announcing the maidens.

"LADY JUNE AGATHA ANNETTE LABELLE OF THE BARON HOUSEHOLD!" the usher called. Prince Sebastian held his breath as a slender woman with blonde curls draped over one of her bare shoulders, wearing a deep orange gown that accentuated her waist and pushed her bust almost to her throat descended the stairs.

She reached the Prince and bowed low, revealing another several inches of cleavage. "Your Highness," she said, a coy smile on her lips. "I hope you find me *pleasurable* company." She bowed again.

"Thank you, Lady June," the Prince gulped. His anxiety seemed to have disappeared as his manhood took control of his brain functions. "You are a delight, I am sure. Uh... How-how do you spend your time?"

"Oh!" Lady June seemed caught off guard by the question. "I... I work with my mother at the Women's Charity League in the city. We raise funds for various causes through high class events and fundraisers!"

"That sounds very meaningful," Prince Sebastian said, surprised by her answer. She had a beautiful face, she seemed youthful and fun-loving, but also serious and dedicated to matters that greatly affected the kingdom's prosperity. She had also made it clear his pleasure was a priority... Yes, she was a viable candidate indeed. But of course, there were many more to come. He gave a slight nod of his head. "Lovely meeting you, Lady June; until we meet again."

"Your *Highness*," she said again, bowing low. Then she turned and joined the crowd of guests encircling the ballroom.

"LADY CHARLOTTE DEIDRE HOLLY LABELLE OF THE BARON HOUSEHOLD!" the usher called.

From the side of the ballroom, by the large crystal bowls of wine and barrels of ale, stood Asche. She watched for almost an hour and each lady was introduced, sometimes a Lady, often a Mistress or Mademoiselle, rarely a Princess. Asche had gasped aloud, drawing looks from those around her at the announcement of "THE PRINCESS WILLOW JAVA RINETTE WILRIGHT OF NOWHORL!" The woman in the golden dress... from the gardens, a *Princess?*

Asche watched as she bowed to the Prince and he reciprocated. After a short exchange she joined her parents on the opposite side of the hall, where the other kingdom's monarchs all had thrones on a raised dais.

The introduction ended with a fanfare of trumpets, then the band struck up a song and the dancing began, overseen by the King from the balcony. Asche was just watching the ushers lead each royal family up to greet the King whilst their children enjoyed the party below, when a voice whispered in her ear, "So you have finally arrived."

10

"Rufus!" Asche said delightedly, holding her upper chest in shock. "Yes! I was late because... I was late, but I am here now," she fumbled.

"You are here now," Rufus agreed. "Shall we dance?"

"I would be delighted! Hopefully I remember how..." she drifted off.

"Never fear," Rufus said grandly, taking her hand and holding his head high. "For I am well versed and shall lead you as no man ever has!"

Asche laughed at his forced gravitas. "No one ever *actually* has!" She followed him onto the dancefloor of the ballroom and they began to move between the other couples dancing, graceful and fluid.

Rufus really was a wonderful dancer. When the music was soft and slow, Rufus led her gently, with purpose; when it became fast and frantic his movements became harder and more chaotic. They danced the hours away, not stopping until the King ordered that the chandeliers and torches be lit when the sun finally started to go down.

"I really should have eaten more at the banquet!" Asche said, fanning herself as the left the ballroom out of one of the many open doors leading out onto a large balcony that overlooked the gardens.

"When did you get here?" Rufus asked. "Was the banquet already over?"

"No, I simply... became distracted by the gardens! They are very beautiful. Have you seen them?"

"I have, in fact. But I could most definitely be persuaded to see them again?" Rufus looked at Asche expectantly.

"Well, *Sir* Rufus," she said with great propriety. "Would you care to escort a Lady to the gardens?"

"Why *Mademoiselle* what an *honour* it would be!" he replied mockingly. They laughed as they made their way to the stone staircase at the far side of the balcony that led down to the courtyard and gardens below.

"I saw the most scandalous thing when I was walking in the gardens earlier this afternoon," Asche told Rufus as they walked.

"Oh?" he asked. "What was that?"

"I was looking amongst the roses. I heard a noise and when I turned a corner I found two women set up on each other... like animals! It was quite scandalous indeed."

"Wow!" Rufus exclaimed. "That certainly paints quite a picture," he said. "What were they doing?"

"Oh," Asche replied. "I-I did not stay to look, of course!"

"Of course you didn't," Rufus said, clearly worried he had caused offence. "I meant what did you see?"

Asche looked up at Rufus and immediately looked away shyly. She was both uncomfortable and invigorated by the conversation. She remembered the look on the two women's faces, the ecstasy they were experiencing. She wondered if she would ever experience something like that.

Asche built up the courage to look at Rufus again. "Well," she began. "They were kissing and her dress had come apart slightly..."

"Go on," Rufus encouraged her.

"Well," Asche went on. "Her breasts were showing," her voice squeaked. "And her skirts were up. The other woman was kissing her down her chest and then she had her hand up her dress."

The two stopped walking as Rufus turned to face Asche directly. He looked her in the eyes as though scrutinising what she had told him. "And how did you feel about coming across two people doing such things?" he asked her.

"Well," Asche giggled nervously. "I-I found it quite moving."

"Moving?"

"These women clearly felt quite passionately about each other and what they were experiencing together was obviously something very dear to them to have them enraptured so," Asche explained.

"I see," Rufus said.

"It...it is something I long for sometimes," Asche admitted softly.

"What?" Rufus laughed. "To be taken asunder among the garden beds?"

"No!" Asche laughed. "I mean to feel so strongly about someone and to have them feel strongly in return. Those acts of passion show great feeling between the two of them. I wish I had someone who loved me as clearly as those two women love each other.

"I see," Rufus said. "But of course, you are aware that there are many people who partake in such activities that have no feelings for each other at all?"

"Yes, I do know this," Asche replied. "I simply like to believe those feelings are out there for me somewhere and that I am meant to live as passionately with someone who cares deeply for me and whom I love dearly in return."

"Mademoiselle, I would not have it any other way." Rufus leaned forward. Asche held her breath expectantly, closing her eyes.

Their lips had almost touched when a loud voice out yelled out behind them, "Your Highness! There you are!"

"What? Where? Asche yelped, looking around.

"Oh no!" Rufus exclaimed. "I-I must see to the Prince!" he said suddenly. "If he is out here then I must return him to the ball at once!"

"What? Are you saying you work *here*? For the *royal family?*"

"In a sense," he answered. "It is my responsibility to ensure the Prince remains where he is meant to be tonight," Rufus said quickly. "But I promise I will see you again. Have a good evening Asche."

Then he was gone. He took off into the night just as two guards raced by calling out, "Your Highness! You must rejoin the ball! The King is asking for you!"

Asche was left standing there in a daze. She shook her head at to rid herself of the shock of what had occurred before slowly making her way back inside to the ball.

Upon entering she saw a gentleman in a red double breasted suit with golden lapels seemingly hiding behind one of the thick velvet curtains. "Are you alright?" she asked.

"Oh! Hello Mademoiselle," he responded. "I am sorry for you to find me in such a childish manner, I am just trying to catch my breath."

"Oh, Your Highness! Asche exclaimed, bowing low. "I am sorry! I did not recognise you! Whatever are you doing hiding behind the curtain, Sire?"

"I am simply trying to regain myself," the Prince answered. "I have not had a single moment to myself since my father announced this festival and while I am most certainly grateful for the opportunity to serve my kingdom as their King, I do find the constant introductions rather tedious."

"I am so sorry," Asche said. "I had no idea, but surely, Sire, you have found *someone* who piques your interest?"

"Potentially," he answered. "And hopefully whoever my selection is, is a wonderful Queen for our fair kingdom as is rightfully deserved by the people, but it certainly does place quite a bit of pressure."

"I understand," Asche sighed. "I mean I most certainly do *not* understand the intricacies of choosing an appropriate person to marry, but I do understand the pressure of doing right by one's family. Have a good evening Sire."

Asche made to leave, but the Prince had other plans. "Wait! Will you dance with me? Just a short one? Anything to keep the guards and my father and the other women at a distance for just ten minutes?"

"Oh! Of-of course Sire, whatever would please you."

"Thank you." The Prince extricated himself from the long velvet curtains and offered his arm to Asche. Together they stepped onto the dance floor and began a simple, slow number.

While she enjoyed herself dancing Asche felt that it simply was not the same with the Prince. Dancing with Rufus was... different. She went through the motions surely enough; they were simple enough for her to follow, but dancing with the Prince simply did not feel the same.

He lacked the sincerity that Rufus had showed her. It was clear that despite the Prince's kind nature, he was simply using her as a means to be left in peace. At the end of the third song Asche made to leave. "Thank you for a wonderful evening Sire," she said. "Thank you very much for the invitation, but I fear it is time for me to go home. It is getting rather late."

"Wait! You cannot leave now!"

"I am sorry, but I have much to do in the morning. I have stayed far later than I expected already."

"But surely you would remain for the Crown Prince?" he said expectantly.

"I am sorry," she replied, genuinely upset. "But I cannot," and she turned and fled from the ballroom, running up the stairs, through the entryway and back down the main stairs to her silver carriage.

Her ex-lizard footmen were ready and waiting. They flung open the doors and quickly helped her climb in just as several guards came arrived and began to call out to her as they ran down the stairs.

"Hurry! We must leave!" Asche called to the once-toad coachman. He flicked the reins, and the ex-mice took off at a gallop, gaining speed the further away from the Palace they ran.

♠

"I want her found!" the Prince ordered. "I *must* know who she is!"

"Your Highness," the guards nodded and ran off.

"Your Highness?" another voice questioned as the Prince paced the entrance hall.

Prince Sebastian looked up. "Can I help you?"

"No, Your Highness. My name is Digby Earnest Baron, of the Baron household," Asche's father introduced himself.

"The Baron household? I do believe it was your daughter to whom I was introduced first?"

"My stepdaughters, yes," Digby corrected. "If I may, Your Highness, are you alright? You seem in quite a state, Sire."

"There was a maiden I was dancing with. She fled the ball before I could get her name."

"The one in the blue gown?"

The Prince's head snapped up. "Do you know her?"

"Oh no... No, Your Highness," Digby Baron insisted, waving his hands. The Prince looked downcast.

Digby felt guilty... for the maiden *had* seemed familiar. But it could not possibly have been... *Asche?*

For many miles Asche could hear the Palace guards on their steeds following her, but there must have been something watching over her tonight ensuring that she was able to slip away. With the many twists and turns on the streets of the city she was finally able to lose the Palace guards, arriving at the very back of the mansion's property where she was able to carefully hide the carriage behind the old weeping willow by the back fence, just a short walk from her mother's grave and her precious hazel tree.

Asche quickly pulled off her dress and stuffed it in the nook of the tree, ensuring that it was safe and hidden until she would need it again... the very next day.

11

Asche been cleaning all morning, since long before dawn. She had to make it appear as though she had been home the previous day, and that meant cleaning as much as she possibly could to make it seem as though she had been busy.

What she wanted to do was rush into Madame Marmorante's shop and talk to the seamstress, not quite sure whether what she had experienced the previous day was real or not and finding that she was demanding proof of herself that the dressmaker was indeed a Fairy Godmother. She had to keep the urge to herself however, just one of the many urges that she had felt since meeting both Madame Marmorante *and* Rufus.

The previous evening had been everything she had ever wanted and more. She only wished that she had been able to spend more time with Rufus, but she had resolved to ensure that she did just that on the second day of the festival, and that meant cleaning as much as she could while she had the opportunity to do so, so she could be on time to the festival this time.

Once she arrived, she would find Rufus immediately and they would spend the day finally exploring the gardens as they had planned to the previous evening, if, of course, the Prince did not go off and disappear again. She hoped that they, too, might be able to explore the gardens a little deeper... maybe not so much as the women she came across the day before, but it was definitely something her mind and heart were open to, and when she thought about what she had found the women doing she found her body buzzing with excitement.

There were only three days of the King's festival and now only two remained. She was not going to let a single moment more go to waste, and so, she scrubbed. She was on her hands and knees in the main foyer cleaning each and every one of the giant marble tiles that lead from the front door all the way to the grand staircase. She moved as quickly as she possibly could without making it appear as though she were rushing, and also trying to ensure that she did not miss a single spot, for both of these things would make it appear as though she had not in fact been cleaning the floors since yesterday, and that is what she needed the Contessa Georgina to believe.

Breakfast had been taken away. The Contessa, June and Charlotte were now upstairs getting ready for the second day of the festival. Today's dresses were just as glamorous as the previous day's. The Contessa Georgina was in a beautiful red number. It had a silken skirt with a long train and a high raised colour with long sleeves that flared out at the elbow.

June was wearing pink. Not the same pink that Charlotte had worn the previous day, but a deep, bright, glowing pink. There were several layers to the skirt, so once the cage was placed underneath, it caused the dress to have such a large circumference that she had to lean over almost double in order to reach anyone. Asche wondered exactly how she planned to dance with the Prince with such voluminous skirts.

Charlotte however was wearing a soft green. It was a pastel lime colour with embroidered lace on the cuffs. Her shoulders were bare and there was a deep forest green ribbon tied around her waist. The remainder of the dress dropped in a silky sheet. It moved like water, following her every movement a half a second after she made it. Asche really did appreciate Charlotte's choices, for they were both beautiful and practical for the summertime heat. She knew that should Charlotte get an offer of marriage at this festival, either from the Prince or someone else, that the person would respect the choices she had made and see her for the fine, logical woman that she was.

Asche found that despite going along with her mother and sisters expectations, Charlotte was quite kind to her, and after having had her mother tell her that kindness was such an important thing in life, it was something she greatly appreciated in everyone, especially Charlotte. Asche knew that Charlotte was almost as trapped as she was herself, for there were expectations of her and how she behaved within the family, just as there was for Asche.

"Good morning Cinderella," a voice came down the stairs.

"Good morning Stepmother!" Asche replied brightly. "Did you sleep well?"

The Contessa regarded Asche, her face blank. "Well enough, and what did you find yourself to do whilst we were away yesterday, Cinderella?"

"Oh, Stepmother, there was quite a lot to do," Asche replied. "I began the floors... which I am only just now managing to complete. I also had to clean up my-my bedroom," she answered, her voice choking slightly at the memory of walking into her room and finding her destroyed dress.

"I also made sure the stables were clean for when the horses returned with the carriage, so they would remain ready for days two and three of the Kings festival," she went on. "And next I plan on emptying out all the fireplaces, so I have collected all of the fireplace tools in readiness for cleaning them."

"Well, well, well... You *have* been a busy girl, haven't you?"

"Yes Stepmother! I promised you that I would show you what dedication I have to this family and I am holding true to my word. I will show you just how much I love and respect you all!"

The Contessa looked down at her from the top of the staircase, watching as Asche turned back to her work of scrubbing the tiles.

"Yes," she said quietly. "See to it that you do." The Contessa turned back around and made her way back down the hallway towards her daughter's rooms.

Asche breathed a sigh of relief. She was grateful that she had not been caught in her lies, but now she had to ensure she followed through and actually completed all of the tasks that she had told the Contessa would be done. She knew she could trust Arina and Heidi with both her plan and the tasks that needed doing, especially since Gerry would not be needed throughout most of the day after he had delivered her Stepmother and stepsisters to the palace.

Asche quickly finished up the floors and made her way down to the kitchens, where Arina and Heidi were standing by the fireplace rather enjoying the fact that they had not had to cook neither lunch nor dinner the day before and the same would happen both today and tomorrow.

"Arina?" Ash began. "Heidi? I need your help."

"Wha' is the matter Dear?" Arina asked. "Is everythin' alrigh'?"

"I hope so. I..." Asche lowered her voice to a whisper. "I attended the King's festival yesterday."

"You did?" Arina exclaimed.

"Shh! I did," Asche said. "And I wish to go today and tomorrow as well...but I shall not be able to if I cannot keep up the ruse of doing chores whilst I remain here at home.

"If-if nothing is being cleaned for the next two days it will become clear that I was not doing anything whilst they were away. That will either get me locked in my room for a week for laziness or they will discover that I have in fact been *attending!*"

"Oooooh!" Heidi said in realisation. "We understand. You need us to get some extra things done around the house."

"If that is at all possible?" Asche answered.

"Of course, Dear!" Arina insisted. "Wha'ever you need us to do, consider i' done!"

Asche gave them the same list that she had given the Contessa Georgina and Heidi immediately made for the upper fireplaces while Arina walked out to the stables. Asche threw herself to the ground in front of the fireplace and began sweeping it out, ensuring not a single speck of soot remained.

She only looked up when she heard Gerry, once again, bringing the horses out of the stables to hitch them to the carriage. Asche came to the kitchen door, the top half of which had been thrown open to let the heat of the fireplace out from breakfast, watching as the Contessa Georgina in her stepsisters, June and Charlotte, climbed into the carriage in their new gorgeous, elaborate gowns.

Charlotte peered out of the window after they had climbed in and gave a little wave. Asche waved back, then watched as the carriage slowly disappeared around the side of the house and back towards the Palace. The moment they were out of sight, Asche rushed back to the fireplace, eager to quickly finish her task so she could bathe, change and get to the palace herself.

After a few minutes of effort and knowing that Gerry would likely not return for an hour at least, she pulled at her dress, yanked it off and threw it to the floor. She had no plans to wear it again that day and she would need to bathe afterwards anyway, so there was no need for her to be wearing it now when all it did was restrict her movement and cause her to sweat all the more as she worked.

The ash and soot were gone from the fireplace, the pot had been polished and cleaned, and all that was left to do was scrub down the brickwork at the back of the giant stone pit. She had just gotten started, black soot on her face, her underclothes almost soaked through from how careless she was being, when there was a gentle cough from behind her. She turned around and found none other... than Rufus.

"Whatever are you doing here?" Asche asked. "How did you know where to find me?"

"Nixie," he answered simply.

"Nixie," Asche repeated, nodding. "She is... *special*, isn't she?"

"I certainly think so," he answered. "But in reality, she is simply a wonderful woman who loves to take care of the people she loves."

"You do not think..." Asche began. "There is something... *magical* about her?"

"Whatever do you mean?" he asked confused.

"Oh, nothing," she waved her hand. "It is nothing. Why are you here? Why did you not wait for me at the palace?"

"Well, it became rather obvious that we can be interrupted quite easily at the palace. I thought that here we would have a little more privacy for ourselves."

"Well," Asche began. "My family have already left for the festival. "I was simply finishing one last task when I made a bit of a mess and-oh!" She suddenly realised that she was still only wearing her underclothes, her dress abandoned on the floor beside her. She lunged down and pulled it off the floor covering herself quickly.

"Please," Rufus said. "You needn't do that on my behalf."

"And if I do it for my own?" Asche retorted.

"Well then, I will allow you all the modesty you desire!" Rufus turned around, giving her the opportunity to clothe herself. Asche made to do just that but paused as she was about to climb into the skirts of her dress.

She once again pictured the women in the garden; how unhindered they were, how little they cared about regulations and expectations about how they should think, feel, and act. She glanced back to Rufus. He still had his back turned to her. Asche let her dress fall back to the floor, stepped out of it, and crossed the kitchen until she was standing right behind him. Then she reached out and took his hand.

Rufus turned around, and once the look of shock had calmed on his face, it was replaced by one of longing. He gazed at her, his face inches from hers. Asche gulped uncertainly, before she rose onto her tiptoes and kissed him softly.

Rufus responded immediately, placing a hand on the side of her face, his fingers lacing through her hair. He kissed her back deeply. Asche threw her arms around his neck as he took his other hand wrapped it around her waist, pulling her close to him so their bodies pressed up against each other.

Asche felt her face grow hot again. She fought the urge to fan her face as the heat moved down, causing her moistening folds to throb longingly. She could feel Rufus thickening against her.

"Asche," he whispered desperately into her ear. He pulled away long enough to reach down and lift her into his arms, carrying her to the bench by the fireplace and laying her gently on the cool stone.

"Rufus," she said breathlessly, as he began to unbutton the front of her undershirt.

He paused. "I am sorry," he said. "Do you want me to stop?"

"No!" she gasped, sitting up and pulling Rufus back to her. Asche kissed him again, letting her hands drop to the waist of his pants. She unbuckled them enough to push her hands deep down, deep enough to grasp his hardened member. Rufus groaned with pleasure.

Rufus's hands moved back to Asche's undershirt, running his fingers along the peaks of her nipples, He had began to grind his hips against her, a moan releasing from her lips as she continued to kiss him.

"Well, wha' do we have here?" Arina's voice said loudly.

Asche gasped, her hands flying back up to her shirt to redo her buttons. Rufus quickly buckled his belt, but his excitement remained clear. "I am sorry Madame," he bowed, his hands covering himself as best he could. "I... I took leave of my senses for a time. I apologise for such disrespect to your household."

"I think i's *her* that should be apologisin' Lad!" she laughed. "Jus' ge' a look a' you! Covered in fireplace soo'!"

Asche looked Rufus' once lovely suit. It was now covered in patches of black and grey, including a large spattering across his cheek. "Oh, Rufus, I *am* sorry!"

"Think nothing of it, my Lady," he insisted, bowing slightly. "I can change simply enough." He moved to the kitchen door, which Arina held open for him. "I shall see you at the festival?" he asked.

"I will be there as soon as I can," Asche promised, climbing down from the stone bench.

"Farewell!" he called to the both of them as he climbed onto one the palace's very own white chargers and disappeared down the drive.

'Well Love, I can see why you wan' to ge' to tha' festival now!" Arina roared with laughter. Asche's face burned with embarrassment.

12

In the palace, Contessa Georgina had joined her husband, June and Charlotte following along behind. "Is it necessary for you to be here the entire three days?" Georgina was asking.

"There is very little point to me returning for only a few hours when I only need to return as soon as the sun has risen," Digby was saying. "With the plans for the wedding and coronation already being executed, I am expected to be here. I certainly would not want to lose my station."

Contessa Georgina sighed. "No, of course not."

"And there are many benefits to remaining here," Digby went on. "Did I tell you about happening upon the Prince after the ball last night?"

June and Charlotte gasped and squealed. "Girls!" Georgina hissed. "Compose yourselves!" She turned back to her husband. "Whatever did he say?"

"He wanted to know the name of the maiden he was dancing with; the one who fled," Digby said.

Georgina groaned. "Harlot! She is the talk of everyone here! Do you know who she is?"

"I... I do not think I do," he answered slowly. "But I *did* happen to tell him of the fine young ladies of the Baron household." He winked at June and Charlotte. "He remembered you."

"He did!" Georgina gasped. "That is most *wonderful* news!" She looked around, searching the faces of the ushers. She had someone she needed to see...

♠

Asche had forgotten her embarrassment by the time she had finished bathing. The moment she was clean she was overcome by excitement. She covered herself with a simple purple frock with elbow length sleeves and ran to the hazel tree.

She gasped in shock when she removed her dress from the nook of the tree; the satin and lace gown she had hidden there was gone, and in its place was one with many layered skirts. It had an embroidered bodice covered in beads and a green peacock feather pattern with delicate gold linework that followed the sleeves to the elbow.

The slippers had also changed... or had been replaced; Asche did not know. The once silver slippers were now an iridescent gold. "Impossible!" Asche exclaimed, but she put them on all the same and made her way to the weeping willow tree and her toad-led carriage.

The lizards, mice and toads were all waiting right where she left them, the coachman and footmen chatting happily about the high protein value found in flies. They fell silent as she approached. "Mistress," the coachman bowed low.

"Thank you Mr Toad," she said. Footman number two open the door and escorted her in. "And you also Mr Lizards."

The carriage made its way through the streets to the palace for the second time. Asche's nerves had left her completely. Today, she felt only excitement. This time she arrived in time to be led up the stairs and through the entryways by the ushers.

It made her feel very official when the usher came to her and asked her name. "Asche Mariella Baron," she said.

"Ah, yes!" the usher said. "The final daughter of the Baron household! Welcome!" he took her arm and led her back into the banquet hall. "Lunch has just been served so everything is still lovely and warm," he informed her. "We are delighted you were able to join us today! I shall see to it that your name is placed on the list for introductions for this evening. Your sisters were announced last night, but-"

"-No!" Asche exclaimed. The usher looked at her, confused. "I-I met the Prince last night. There really is no need for another introduction."

"Mademoiselle, the introduction is not simply for the Prince, but the entire royal family! Surely you would like King Hugo and the royal court to know who you are should the Prince claim you as his choice?"

"Oh I highly doubt that will be the case, Sir," she sighed. "After speaking with him last night, it... it appears he has his sights on another."

The usher raised his eyebrows in surprise. "Well... *that* is certainly news! He did not happen to mention... a name?"

"Uh... not-not directly... but I feel he was implying that it was a member of my own family... as to not... offend me," Asche lied.

"Of course," the usher said, nodding sagely.

"Yes," Asche went on. "Should the unexpected occur, I can make the proper introductions then, I am sure."

"Yes, of course," the usher nodded, bowing as she released his arm. "Have a wonderful day Mademoiselle."

Asche made her way down the stairs, heading for the same cake table from yesterday. If there were two things she was not going to stop herself from getting her hands on during this festival, one of them were these cakes. "You are not seriously back *again!*" a voice hissed across from her.

Charlotte.

"Whatever is the matter?" Asche asked. "I was able to come yesterday without issue. Why not come again? It is a once in a lifetime opportunity!"

"Because you are giving me *hives!*" Charlotte snapped, her cheeks indeed looking quite red in contrast with her light green gown. "The more you are here the *harder* it will become to keep you hidden! And don't think I did not see you dancing with the Prince last night!"

Asche froze, terrified. "But... but that did not *mean* anything, I swear to you! He simply wanted peace away from everyone and thought dancing with me, who was *completely* disinterested, would assuage the crowd and the King!" she explained. "Did the Contessa see?"

"*Everybody* saw!" Charlotte exclaimed under her breath, clearly wishing she was able to yell. "You are all anybody is talking about! Mother is suspicious already! She recognised you I am *sure* of it! Why do you think she questioned you this morning?"

"Oh no!" Asche whispered. "Charlotte, this is not what I wanted... but *please*, I have met someone and it is *them* I wish to see. Please Charlotte, do not say anything!"

"The ball tonight is to be a masque," she spat. Then she took a calming breath. "Make to sure you get a hold of one the moment they are brought around and until then, *see to it that you are not seen!*" Charlotte took two steps away and disappeared into the crowd.

Asche did exactly the same as she had the previous day; she took a handful of the small delicious cakes and headed for the garden.

♠

The Contessa, in her silken red gown, was once again with the usher. "Come now Simon, you must know something? What has the Prince said? Even a whisper?"

The usher, Simon, looked down through the high collar, to the smooth skin of the Contessa's chest, pushed high from the tightness of her corset. "Well, Madame... perhaps I have heard something..."

"Oh?" Georgina said expectantly, her smile growing. She moved closer to him, running her finger delicately on the shiny silver buckle of his pants. "And whatever do you need to feel comfortable to share such important and valuable secrets?"

Usher Simon appeared thoughtful, before taking the Contessa's hand delicately and leading her into the deserted palace library. Rows and rows of books lined every inch of the walls, save for where ornate silver spiral staircases led to the upper floor of the library, which held plush chaise lounges and yet more walls covered in books.

Simon lifted the Contessa and placed her gently on one of the cushioned lounges, sliding his hands up her legs, revealing her complete lack of underclothes. He slowly kissed his way from her ankle to her mound, feeling the slick wetness beneath his lips.

Georgina began to moan as Simon's tongue explored her in her entirety. "I am surprised this is what would please you enough to share what you know," she panted as her heart pounded from the rush of the blood.

Simon responded by moving his lips and tongue further back, far past where she normally entertained men, lifting her hips as to gain greater entry. Georgina yelped at the sensation. Simon pulled back. "Forgive me Madame... Might a gentleman be so bold?"

Georgina weighed her options, thinking of the possible ramifications of both choices. She came to the conclusion that the benefits far outweighed any possible cost. "A *gentleman* need not ask," she finally answered, taking hold of his collar and leading him back to her.

Simon stopped. He took Georgina by the hips and turned her over, leaning her over the back of the chaise. He then unbuckled his pants, sliding them to his knees, before bringing the Contessa's skirts up over her head. He wanted to watch *everything*.

He licked one of his fingers and gently pressed it to the other hole, eliciting a shudder from the Contessa. He pushed harder, letting his finger slide in further. Georgina moaned softly. He removed his fingers, grasping his hardened member and leading it to the tight button.

He experienced a little resistance, before it gave way completely and his shaft slid into her. Georgina cried out. Simon paused. "Are you sure you are alright?"

"Yes," she answered immediately. "Do... not... stop."

Simon rocked back and forth, gently sliding in and out of her taut, round buttocks. When the movements became easier, as his shaft became slick from the saliva he had left behind, he began to move faster. Georgina gripped the back of the chair, her breathing becoming heavier and heavier as Simon moved faster.

This certainly was *not* how Georgina would have chosen to favour the usher, but when his thrusts gained momentum, to the point of slamming into her with such ferocity that she was being pushed further into the cushions of the chair, she was practically screaming with pleasure as a rush of energy ignited deep in the core of her womanhood and her wetness flowed freely down her thighs. The rush continued, then almost doubled when Simon threw himself over the top of her, moving even faster still, until he began to moan almost as loudly as she.

Georgina felt everything tighten again as Simon's organ began to pulse within her, almost exploding out of her with the force of his release. Georgina succumbed again as waves of pleasure overcame her body, for despite seeing himself to fruition, Simon continued to thrust deeply into her, not stopping until had become flaccid and still.

Georgina rolled back over to face Simon as he pulled his pants back to his waist and buckled them back up. "Well... I feel like that is most definitely a bargain well struck," she said, fanning her face while she resettled her dress into place.

"Quite Madame, quite," he nodded, still breathing heavily.

"So tell me... what does the Prince have in his mind?"

"You recall the maiden he danced with in the blue gown last night?"

"I do. No one has been able to say who she is or where she is from; is she from our kingdom or another? She appears suddenly as a phantom and is gone again just as quickly! What do you know about her?"

"Nothing," Simon answered simply. Georgina shot him an irritated look.

"But I hear from a very reliable source that *she* is of no interest to the Crown Prince... unless of course she happens to be one of your daughters."

Georgina perked up. "How do you mean?" she asked earnestly.

"Well, I have been told by someone who spoke *directly* with him that Prince Sebastian *heavily* implied he had taken interest in a daughter of the Baron household.

"A daughter of the *Baron* household?" she repeated, panic rising. She could have sworn she had seen Cinderella at the ball the previous night, but that was not possible? She had clearly done far too much at the mansion to have had the time to also attend the ball? And the dress had been destroyed! Surely there was no way she had such a beautiful gown simply *lying around?*

"Yes," Simon said cheerily. "Either June or Charlotte are currently under the Prince's eye! Is it not marvellous?"

"June or Charlotte *specifically?*" Simon nodded. Georgina sighed with relief. "Who is so reliable? Who told you this marvellous news?"

"Why, your Stepdaughter of course! Lady Asche!"

Cold hatred clawed back into Georgina's heart. She looked at Simon, who all but cowered. *"Where is she?"*

13

Asche was still exploring the gardens. She had been looking through the different colours of lilies for almost an hour in an attempt to follow Charlotte's advice and avoid the rest of the guests. She also thought that if Rufus was going to find her then the gardens would be the first place he would think to look.

Her assumption proved correct. Just as she was reaching up from smelling a yellow bloom, movement caught the corner of her eye. She turned towards it and found Rufus, grinning at her from ear to ear.

"So, we meet again," Asche said.

"Indeed, we do," he replied. "Would you care to take a walk with me?"

"Definitely." Asche and Rufus meandered through the gardens.

Once they reached the highest of the hedges, the ones that grew so tall they were over their heads, Rufus took hold of Asche's hips and guided her to the leafy wall. He kissed her fiercely as though it had been years since they had seen each other last rather than hours.

"I am sorry that we were not able to finish what we began this morning," Asche whispered.

"Luckily, there is very little chance will be caught out here with the events of the day being sporting events. Most of the partygoers will be on the other side of the Palace by the tennis courts and polo fields," Rufus explained.

"So...?"

"Yes," Rufus gave a slow nod. Asche kissed him again. He kissed her back feverishly, as if she were all that were left in existence. He pulled at the buttons that ran down the back of her dress, undoing them one by one until slowly the front of the bodice came down revealing her bare chest.

Asche was nervous. No one had ever gazed at her way Rufus was at this moment. How did she compare to the others he must have seen?

Rufus noticed her discomfort. "Is everything alright?" he asked.

"I fear I feel quite... inadequate," Asche explained. She looked away in embarrassment.

Rufus took her chin in his fingers and tilted her face back towards his. "You could never be anything but perfect to me," he told her.

"I am sorry," Asche sighed, her hands covering her eyes. "I have ruined the mood."

"Never," he replied. "However if you are unsure as to whether you wish to continue, then we could always go and explore the Palace?" he suggested. "It will be deserted given everyone will be at the sporting grounds."

"Me? See the palace? That would be a dream come true!" she replied.

"Then I would gladly escort you, My Lady," he told her as she quickly did up her dress. He led Asche back through the gardens, up the stairs to the ballroom balcony and from there, down a wide sweeping hallway that led to the upper floors.

Asche needn't have feared being found out, for June's moment had come. She had sidled up to the Prince at the banquet, bowing low enough to share her entire bosom with him. He had responded by asking if she would like to take a walk, to which June had readily accepted.

As a result, Georgina was skulking around the second floor royal quarters, listening to the pleasured moans and cries of Prince Sebastian taking her eldest daughter. She was there for well over an hour, the noises drifting out of the Prince's personal quarters relentlessly.

Georgina was thrilled. Everything was working out perfectly. Even if it turned out that upstart orphan *was* the maiden in the blue gown, both she and Digby had directed the Prince directly to her daughters, and here the Prince was, showing a clear intimate desire for June. Yes... everything was coming along nicely. Cinderella could wait.

♠

Asche was amazed; the long red carpet runners that lined every hallway, the wonderfully intricate paintings that hung on the walls, the beautiful ceramic pottery that sat on delicate stands down one side of the hallways while a number of suits of armour lined the walls opposite.

"What would you like to see?" Rufus asked her.

Asche looked around, raising her hands. "Everything!" she laughed. "I have watched the palace since I was a small child from my window. I never thought in all my life that I would actually have the chance to see it!"

"Then everything it is!" Rufus replied. He showed her the large formal dining hall and every gallery on all four storeys.

They peeked into the library, where Asche gaped at just how many books they could manage to hold within one space.

On the upper storey Rufus led Asche out through a door at the top of a long spiral staircase and onto the roof. Asche's breath caught in her throat "This is spectacular!"

From the top of the roof it was as though they could see the entire kingdom. The forests to the left of the palace that the royals used for hunting began at the polo grounds and travelled all the way to the next kingdom. Asche could see that the polo match was still happening. She watched as Prince Sebastian rode on his black stallion, scoring to the delight of the crowd. All of the maidens clapped and cheered.

"You must come face to face with the Prince quite a lot," Asche said.

"Yes I do," he answered. "Why?"

"I only ask because he took fancy to one of the women on the first night of the ball. He told me so–"

"–He did?"

"Yes. I thought he might be talking about... about someone I know," Asche stopped herself quickly, unwilling to discuss her family. "I would hope that he would be a good husband to her if that were the case."

"Oh!" Rufus said, seemingly relieved. "You can rest assured that Prince Sebastian is utterly committed to doing right by the kingdom and he thoroughly plans on only selecting a Queen that will be perfect for them," Rufus said. "I am sure that any selection will be treated with the highest respect and regard."

"That is good," Asche said. To the right of the palace, on the opposite side to the polo fields and the hunting forest, the city sprawled out in front of them; houses and rooves of every shape, colour and type disappeared into the distance until they disappeared into the sparkling sea at the very tip of the horizon. "You know, I do believe I can see my house from here," Asche announced.

"Do you think so?" Rufus asked.

"Why yes!" Asche said, pointing. "See? Can you see that steeple just there? That is the very tower from which I have watched the palace all my life," Asche told him. "It is very calm and peaceful up there," she told him.

They made their way down the large spiral staircase and back onto the fourth storey of the palace. The carpet was the same green as the ribbon on Charlotte's dress that evening. Asche looked at it as they walked back down the mile long hallway, keeping her head down. "Rufus, what are the rooms up here?" she suddenly asked.

"These are all bedrooms. They rarely get used unless there are visiting dignitaries," he explained. "It is much too far to travel all the way from the lower floors. The royals are all situated on the second floor. It is only when the palace is at full capacity that anybody is ever up here." He turned and winked at her. "Unless of course you are like us and on an adventure or are heading to the roof for the view!"

"Then... there is no chance of us being interrupted up here?" she suggested.

Rufus paused, a smile playing on his lips. "No," he said slowly. "I suppose not."

"Then would you care to show me what is behind one of these doors?"

Rufus looked from the open window to their left then back to the ornate gilded doors to their right. "The ball will be starting soon," he said uncertainly.

"Oh! Do you wish to attend?"

Rufus let his grin grow before stepping quickly to the right, opening the door and bowing low. "Definitely not."

The evening ball was indeed beginning. Loud trumpets rang out just as Asche disappeared through the doorway and Rufus carefully closed the door. People were making their way into the ballroom as Rufus was reaching down to lift Asche delicately, carrying her to the giant full poster bed on the opposite wall.

By the time the royal family had taken their places in the upper balcony, and King Hugo had greeted his visitors for the second night, Asche's dress had been removed and discarded, thrown haphazardly onto the floor by the bed. As Prince Sebastian made his way back down the stairs to the ballroom floor, taking his place by the usher's side, Asche and Rufus disappeared under the covers of the bed.

Nobody heard the light gasps and low moans as the music began in the ballroom below. Nobody heard the movement of their bodies or how heavy their breathing became as the dancing began and the Prince set off around the room for his nightly pleasantries. Nobody heard as they drove each other to climax, as far below, in the ballroom, Contessa Georgina was on the hunt.

14

Asche and Rufus came out of the bedroom still pulling up their clothes, Asche fixing her skirts and Rufus having to rebutton his double breasted jacket in order to get them to align properly. Asche's hair was still askew; she smoothed down her flyaway hairs as they walked.

"I have never felt such sensations!" she said, laughing. She sighed, taking Rufus' hand "I feel I could spend every moment of my life with you," she told him.

"Is that a proposal, Mademoiselle?" he asked playfully.

"No! I simply mean that what I have experienced with you is far greater than anything else I have ever experienced in my life. Do you understand?"

"I do," he answered. "I have spent many of my days only ever doing what was requested of me by my Masters, having very little choice for myself," he explained. "The time I have spent with you here in these past few days is one of the only times I have truly chosen for myself," he told her. "It would be wonderful to see it last for longer than three days of the King's festival."

They slowly made their way down the three flights of stairs to the ballroom, where, upon entering, Rufus carefully selected two fancy lace masks and offered one to Asche. Asche's was the same peacock blue colour of her dress with beautiful golden edging. Rufus took a black one for himself, placing it carefully over his eyes, before offering his hand to Asche. "Shall we dance?" he asked.

She answered by taking his hand and Rufus led her onto the floor of the ballroom. The music was soft and lilting, perfect for the mood Asche found herself feeling. She truly believed that Rufus was important and special and she would spend all of her days with him if she could... but she was also aware that these three days were quite different to how she lived every other day of her life.

It seemed the same kind of fantasy that she dreamed of, watching from her attic tower window as a child. How is it possible that she could see herself having a future with Rufus when in just another twenty four hours her life would return to what it had always been? She could not possibly be thinking that she could go off with Rufus and live her life leaving her family behind, could she? More than likely the day after tomorrow she would wake just before dawn as normal and go about her chores as she had done every day for the past fifteen years of her life... since just a week after the Contessa Georgina had moved in with her daughters.

Asche and Rufus danced for hours, before finally the music began to slow and King Hugo once again came to the balcony. "GOOD EVENING TO ALL IN ATTENDANCE! On this, the second night of the festival, we hold a masque to take away the pressures of one's identity, to allow people to get to know one another on a deeper level than *what we see!* Please, use this as an opportunity to get to know one another, as it is my hope that whomever my son chooses for his Queen is witty, charming and intelligent, for these qualities are far more defining than what lies behind the masks! NOW, GO FORTH! EAT! *DANCE!*"

The crowd clapped and cheered at the King's words before he took a step back from the balcony and took his seat in his throne. Once again the other royal dignitaries from the neighbouring kingdoms had joined him up in the balcony. Asche could see the Princess Willow of Nowhorl from her place down with the crowd, this time wearing an elegant blue and white gown embroidered from the top of her high collar to the tips of her long sleeves and all the way to where it touched the floor.

After Rufus and Asche had politely applauded the King, Rufus led her out onto the balcony that looked over the gardens as he had the day before.

"The Prince shall begin his dances soon," he told her. "I-I have had a wonderful time with you today Asche," he told her. "However, it is reaching the time where I must return to my Masters. I am sure they must be wondering where I have gotten to," he explained.

"So... this is goodbye for but another evening?"

"I can assure you that I shall be waiting when your carriage arrives tomorrow," he promised her.

"See to it that you do," she replied. "Many areas of the palace have been left unexplored," she smiled conspiratorially.

Rufus threw his head back and laughed. "Oh Asche, I have not had the chance to connect with someone as I have you."

Asche paused. "I am saddened to hear it," she said. "You are a wonderful man who deserves loving people in your life."

Rufus kissed her hand, then Asche was left on the balcony blushing as Rufus made his way back into the ballroom, disappearing into the crowd. Asche gazed out over the gardens thinking about what Rufus said. Could he love her? Truly? Asche was overcome with the idea. It was absolute nonsense, she told herself.

Rufus was a man who worked for the royal family of all people. He lived his life in the palace around the Princes and Princess. There was no possible way there was a future for either of them if they attempted to remain together. She could not possibly leave her family. She had lied to the Contessa Georgina, but she still saw her as a mother and she wanted to please her and show her that she was in fact committed and dedicated to serving her family; of being a part of that family. She was not going to abandon them. They needed her.

Ash walked back into the ballroom, her mask still covering her eyes. It was quite liberating to be able to move amongst the people without the fear of being recognised. She was able to wander through the people looking into the faces to see whether or not she recognised any of them herself.

In the far corner she could still see Charlotte in her beautiful lime green gown with the Forest Green sash, talking to what appeared to be one of the ushers. The usher was laughing uproariously, seemingly taken by something Charlotte had said to him. Charlotte was smiling back. She seemed to be truly enjoying herself. The smile she had on her face was nothing like the ones she would have when she was out attending events with her mother and sister. Here she was able to truly be herself and get to know people on her own terms. Asche was pleased that by doing this she had found someone who enjoyed her as she was.

Asche was just making her way to the other side of the room where long trestle tables had been laid out with food from the banquet earlier in the day when a hand took hers. "Mask or not, I still know that is you," a voice said.

Asche gasped. "Your Highness! How-how are you enjoying your evening Sire?"

"Much better now," he told her. "You would not do me the great service of finishing our dance from last night would you?" he asked.

"I *am* sorry that I had to leave so abruptly," she explained to him. "The duties that I have at home are quite important. I cannot simply disregard them for the sake of dancing," she explained, though it simply came out like excuses.

"Well," he began. "Luckily, we have this evening also and tomorrow evening besides," he said. "I did find it quite the relief to be able to simply dance without speaking or without having to offer idle chit chat to each and every single maiden," he explained. Asche gave him a curious look. "I *do* appreciate being able to get to know each one before making a selection," he went on, offering his hand. "It is just so incredibly exhausting and so when you appear, it is almost like I am being given a break. I greatly appreciate that, so thank you."

"It is an honour to assist," Asche told him graciously, taking his hand. They danced around the ballroom, Asche noticing the eyes on her this time. Charlotte had told her that people were watching the previous night and that no one could keep their eyes off them, but it was more apparent to her this time.

With each twist and turn of the dance, more and more eyes were upon her, until finally she could stand it no longer. "I am sorry Sire, however it is time I take my leave," she told him.

"No, not again! Please stay just a little later this time, won't you? Please?" he practically begged as she headed for the stairs.

"Oh! I will dance with you Your Highness-!"

"-No, Your Highness! Dance with me!"

The women gave Asche the perfect cover as she dodged through body after body, making her way for the stairs.

"CINDERELLA!" She heard a voice screech behind her. Georgina. Asche did not slow down. Asche reached the top step before the first guard attempted to stop her. She ducked under his arm and ran down the hallway and through the banquet hall.

"*STOP HER!*"

Asche turned back in time to see the Prince Sebastian pointing at her from the other side of the banquet hall. She gasped, running as fast as her skirts would allow, through the entrance hall, down the stairs and into her waiting carriage "*GO! Drive!*" she screamed to the coachman. The lizard footmen slammed the door and leapt onto the back of the carriage just before they were left behind as the coachman flicked the reins and the horses broke into a gallop.

Asche was in trouble and she knew it. Her Stepmother had recognised her, despite the mask. Nothing was going to save her now.

This time the carriage took almost an hour to finally return to its place behind the weeping willow. It had needed to change direction over and over in order to outpace the palace guards. When it finally came to a stop, the mice-horses were exhausted, Asche throwing her arms around each one gratefully. She removed her shoes and gown, hiding them in the nook of the hazel tree for the second time.

Asche ran through the kitchen door and right into the Contessa. "Stepmother!" she exclaimed. "I can expl-!"

"-I WILL *NOT* HEAR IT!" Georgina roared, grabbing Asche by her hair and yanking her head back. "You... who have been a *thorn* by your *very existence* since the moment I arrived in this *hovel*... you *dare* to court the Prince?" The Contessa was dragging her across the kitchen, to the door to the left of the stairs.

"No!" Asche cried out painfully. "I wasn't, I *swear!*"

"*LIAR!*"

"He wanted a break from the others! That is all! He told me himself that he had taken interested in another!"

Georgina spun Asche around to face her. "June? Charlotte?"

"He did not say."

"Useless!" Georgina spat, opening the door that led to the cellar and throwing her inside. "If you think for one minute that you will be attending tomorrow, think again!" She slammed the door behind her, and Asche heard the tell tale clicks of the padlock. "If any of you so much as *touch* that door, I shall see to it that you are whipped! *Understood?*"

Hard clicks of the Contessa's heels slowly disappeared, before there was a soft voice at the door. "Oh, Love... I am so sorry..."

Ashe settled herself onto a bag of rice, and wept.

Conte Digby Earnest Baron was once again with the Prince. The ball had ended, the guests had returned home, and every courtier had been requested to present themselves before the royal family.

"I want her found!" Prince Sebastian was saying. "She has the potential to very well be the next Queen of our kingdom and I cannot make such an important decision if I do not know *who she is!*"

"We understand, Your Highness," one of the Barons bowed. "We shall cast our nets a wide as possible."

"Calm yourself, Son," King Hugo said. "We have people from every kingdom attending this festival. We will find her. It will simply be a matter of time."

Digby bit his lip, his suspicion rising as a hard knot settled in his stomach.

15

The sun rose on the morning of the final day of the festival, but the most Asche could see of it was a chink of light between the door hinges and the frame. She had lain awake crying until just before dawn, when her exhaustion had finally taken her and she had fallen asleep.

She was jerked awake with by cellar door being slammed open. Asche blinked sleepily, struggling to see in the light after being kept so long in the dark.

We are leaving now," the Contessa snapped. "If you behave and are *unbelievably* lucky, I might just consider releasing you when I wake in the morning." Then she slammed the door closed again, locking it behind her. "SHE IS *NOT* TO BE FED!" Georgina yelled to Arina or Heidi, Asche could not tell.

It did not matter; Asche could not eat even if she were given the opportunity. She laid back down on the sack of rice, desolate, staring ahead of her into the darkness.

♠

"Vladimir!" Prince Sebastian was calling as he opened his brother's door. "Are you awake?"

"Yes Brother!" he responded coming from his bath still draped in a towel. "You seem rather dreary! I take it you did not sleep well?"

"Oh and you did?"

"I most certainly did! I have been having a wonderful time at the festival! So has Zarina, as it turns out! I think she has met someone," he winked. "Father is finally having a good time, talking of the old times with the other Kings. It appears the only one who is *not* having a good time is you! Despite the fact that at the end of it all, you shall have a Queen, a crown and a kingdom!"

"I am overwhelmed, Vladimir," he told him. "Meeting what feels like every woman in existence and being expected to pick one? I have to evaluate who will fit in with the family, and the kingdom and my *plans*."

"Plans?" Vladimir repeated.

"For the kingdom!" Sebastian said. "She needs to be able to cultivate a family and be diplomatic with other kingdoms *and* have the same aims for the growth and prosperity of our people!"

"Ah. Noble of you," Vladimir said. "To be so analytical as to ensure a match for everyone and not just yourself. I haven't even *heard* you mention a beautiful face or supple breasts. That *is* something."

"Those qualities can be found in *any* maiden," Sebastian scoffed. "Why, I had quite the evening with one just last night! But a *Queen*? She has to have something... more."

Vladimir shook his head in distaste. "You fear not having the time to meet the right maiden, yet waste what time you *do* have with meaningless frivolities?" he scolded his brother. "Sebastian, you have one night left. The wedding is *tomorrow*. Make your introductions tonight and as soon as they are over, go and *find* those that had genuinely sparked something in you! See if there is something more when you speak to them again. Start the process of narrowing down the selection." He clapped his hands on his older brother's shoulder. "Maybe you will feel better once the pool is decidedly smaller."

"Maybe," Sebastian went quiet, then shook himself slightly. "Wait, what is this about *Zarina* meeting someone? Who is he?"

♠

"We would see our daughter become Queen," the King of Nowhorl was saying. He and his wife, as well as their daughter, Princess Willow, were having breakfast with King Hugo and Princess Zarina.

"I agree," Zarina said, receiving a gracious smile in return from the Queen of Nowhorl. "Princess Willow is absolutely the stand out choice for heading a royal household and taking the role of Queen. She is poised, dignified, well educated; we would be most lucky indeed to welcome her into our family."

"Thank you, Zarina!" Willow smiled.

"We thank *you* for attending, despite no betrothal!" Zarina went on. "However, while *we* would most certainly endorse a marriage between our families, we do believe that the final choice is one the Crown Prince should make for himself. It is only right that matters of the heart should be decided by the heart," she finished.

Princess Willow placed a hand on Zarina's. "I could not agree more! I could not bear the idea that I should come into a marriage with anyone who does not truly love me." She shook her head as she looked at the plate in from of her. "The very idea!"

"It does seem rather pointless to have come with no guarantee," the King of Nowhorl grumbled.

"But Sire!" Zarina said. "We consider you and your fair kingdom family already! Whatever would a marriage to Prince

Sebastian provide for either of our kingdoms that we cannot provide you as our allies? Any treaty or trade agreement or aid could most definitely be negotiated *without* an arranged marriage! Let us try!" Zarina insisted. "What is a need you find your kingdom requiring? What is it that we can do to aid our family's kingdom in their quest? Name it and if it is within our power, we shall see it done, such is the respect we have for you, Sire, and your wonderful Queen and Princess."

The King of Nowhorl was looking at her in amazement. "The absolute *gall* of this one!" He began to laugh uproariously. "A tongue so gilded must be unmercifully heavy!" He turned to King Hugo. "You must have you hands full with this one!"

"I most certainly do," King Hugo answered, winking at Zarina. "But I would not have it any other way." He held her hand lovingly. "She is far more eloquent and diplomatic than I could ever be, and she will provide a great service to my son when he is crowned as King. She is also correct; I am adamant that Prince Sebastian be allowed the opportunity for choice, but whether that choice is Princess Willow or not should not determine the relationship we have between our two kingdoms. Tell us we can do strengthen our kingdom's bonds and we will see it done."

The King of Nowhorl nodded, a look of satisfaction on his face. "You are right. Since the war our kingdoms have been quite close."

"Yes, I suppose that we simply presumed there would be a marriage *because* of that relationship," the Queen continued. "One cannot go through what we have together without creating a bond, but I can definitely agree that if political relations can be kept just as strong as they are while also allowing our children to marry for love, then we would be doing what is expected as monarchs as well as parents and that is definitely something I can stand by."

"And of course, there is always Vladimir," the King pointed out, placing his hand on his wife's.

King Hugo nodded. "Oh, I most *definitely* see Princess Willow becoming a member of our family one way or another," Zarina agreed, nodding matter of factly.

♠

The banquet of the final day of the festival was beginning; the guests were arriving steadily, each led in by the attentive ushers. The moment Contessa Georgina entered the banquet hall, wearing a fitted black gown with off the shoulder sleeves, she made for her husband, who was already eating from one of the tables. "Digby!" she hissed.

"Georgina!" he exclaimed. "You look simply ravishing!" He kissed her cheek.

"Not *now* Digby!" she snapped. "What did the Prince say when the ball ended? He and June had quite the encounter last night! Did he mention it at all?"

"He was rather distracted," the Conte answered. "He demanded we find out who the maiden in the blue gown is."

"*Her?*" Georgina hissed venomously. "That hazardous little *leech?*"

"Do you know who she is?" Digby asked, shocked. He knew that his wife had felt threatened by his daughter since they had married, as she represented the life he had lived with his previous wife, Victoria. She had never admitted her disdain so openly.

"No! No, I do not," she answered hastily, waving a hand. "I simply find it irritating that despite the picture that is being painted between the Prince and June, that he remains so curious about this... *tramp!*"

"I am *sure* that the Prince will make the right decision when the time comes," Digby said. "Just wait and see. Now, let us see to the festivities!"

"I have to see to the girls," she answered, waving him off. "And check in with my source..." she whispered under her breath, heading directly for the line of ushers by the entrance hall.

Rufus was dressing into his formal suit for the final day of the festival. This was the day. He could not make any further delays. It had been made clear to everyone in the palace that Prince Sebastian had his eyes set on the maiden in the blue gown... on Asche.

Rufus had to ensure that did not happen. He could not bear to watch her marry the Prince and become Queen... He was sure that was not what she wanted; why else would she have run from him the past two nights and been meeting with him besides?

That was why Rufus had made a decision. He was going to wait with the ushers at the stairs from the very moment people started to arrive. When Asche finally did he was going to open her carriage door himself, introduce himself properly as her escort, laying himself bare for all in attendance to see. Then, he was going to propose. If all went as planned, Prince Sebastian would have no choice but to select another maiden, and he would be free to love Asche for remainder of his days.

It seemed to Rufus the perfect plan, but what he did not expect was to not have the opportunity to enact it. He waited, butterflies in his stomach as the first carriage arrived, then the second, then the third. After the twentieth he developed a rhythm that found him calmer and less anxious.

His heart leapt when he saw three women exit a gold and white carriage, one wearing black, another in white satin with large upper sleeves and layered skirts... and finally the third in a long royal blue gown with a corseted bodice, caped train and embroidered green sleeves. He released his breath however when he saw that it was clearly not Asche.

And so he waited... and waited... and waited.

16

Asche remained right where the Contessa had left her. Throughout the day she would come out of her stupor from time to time due to the banging on the cellar door. Arina, Heidi and Gerry had been working tirelessly all day to free her, to no avail.

"Just stop!" Asche had called out. "It is no use!"

They continued to come at the door with whatever tools they had at their disposal, short of attempting to smelt the locks and hinges, which risked a fire they may not be able to save her from.

It was almost nightfall by Asche's reckoning, based on her tiny sliver of light through the door jam, when the banging stopped and the voices disappeared. The rumbling of her belly had long since ended, seemingly having given up trying to tell her to eat, not that she was interested in opening one of the wine casks or eating dry rice or flour, even if she had been within her senses enough to realise the Contessa would not possibly be able to tell if she had.

Good she thought to herself. *Now I can rest.*

She was wrong.

Suddenly on the other side of the door came half a dozen voices, all yelling at once. It took quite some time for Asche to focus amidst the haze of her hunger and disorientation enough to make sense of what she was hearing.

"Who *are* you?" she heard Heidi shout.

"You be'er ge' ou' o' here!" Arina screeched.

"Mistress!" another voice called out.

"Lady Asche!" she heard another call.

"Mister Lizards?" she yelled, suddenly alert, getting to her feet. She wobbled dangerously, almost as though she had forgotten how to walk. "*IS THAT YOU?*"

"Yes Mademoiselle! We are here to rescue you!" That was Mr Toad

"Rescue her?" Heidi yelled. "Who *are* you?"

"It is alright!" Asche called out to them. "Let them help! Please! Mr Lizards! Mr Toad! Is the Fairy Godmother there? Is Nixie with you?"

"No Mistress!" Mr Toad called through the door. "She has sent us in her stead! But never fear, we will release you!"

"How?"

"STAND BACK!"

Asche threw herself to the floor just in time, before the door exploded off its hinges. When the dust settled, Asche saw Mr Toad standing in the doorway. He looked incredibly round and bulbous, though as she watched, he seemed to be... deflating. "Once a toad, always a toad," he nodded, straightening his bow tie.

Arina and Heidi rushed in and helped Asche out into the kitchen, where they gave her tea and porridge. As she ate and drank she slowly felt the warmth returning to her fingers and toes. "Thank you," she whispered, laying her head on Arina's shoulder.

"I's no' the time to res' now, Lass!" she said, straightening Asche in her chair. "You have go' to ge' to tha' ball!"

"What?" Asche exclaimed. "That is the *last* thing on my mind!"

"You do not understand my dear, we saw what Lady June was wearing when she left," Heidi explained. "She was in a *blue gown!*"

"So?"

"Do you not understand?" Heidi asked. "She means to trick the Prince! You have to warn him!"

"She is pretending... to be me?" Asche asked. Arina and Heidi nodded.

"But... but I do not *want* to marry the Prince! I do not wish to *be* Queen!" she insisted.

"Maybe no' Lass," Arina sighed. "Bu' you can' le' the poor boy go off an' marry her because of a lie!"

Asche looked at her hands, which still held her teacup. She placed it on the kitchen bench. "You are right. I must at least make sure he knows the truth. He has been quite gracious to me, most appreciative for the time he is not being disturbed. I owe him that." Asche got to her feet. Let us see what Nixie has in store for me tonight."

"Who is Nixie?" Heidi asked, as Asche, the toad and the lizards made their way to the hazel tree.

The ball had begun. Prince Sebastian was being introduced to the last of the maidens. When the final name was called and the Prince had briefly spoken to the fine young lady, the trumpets rang out again and the music began. Prince Sebastian immediately made for the staircase that led up to the upper balcony, practically ran up the stairs to where King Hugo sat with Princess Zarina. "She was not announced!" he exclaimed.

"You are sure?" Zarina asked, frowning. "*Every* maiden was to be announced?"

"Yes, but she was not announced either of the nights before and I searched every face; none of them were hers!"

"Maybe she hid her identity, for fear of being overlooked due to her station?" King Hugo suggested. "I believe I made myself clear that all were welcome, but perhaps it is not so clear to the people as I thought?"

"No, that cannot b-"

"-There!" Zarina suddenly gasped, pointing.

Sebastian followed her finger... to a blonde woman in the most exquisite royal blue gown he had ever seen in his life.

♠

Rufus was in an upper hallway overlooking the ballroom. He had finally resigned himself to the fact that Asche would not be attending after the carriages stopped arriving completely and he had continued his vigil for an hour longer than that. He watched the dancers as they moved in time, with perfect synchronicity.

He watched as Prince Sebastian appeared on the floor, crossing as quickly as the crowd would allow him to. He stopped at the woman in the Royal blue dress that Rufus had mistaken for Asche upon her arrival. "Sorry, Prince Sebastian," he sighed. "I made the same mistake; it is not her."

Prince Sebastian, however, seemed to not be swayed. He either was not aware that he had the wrong woman or he did not care. He took her hand and they began to dance. Rufus continued his watch. Another hour past; his eyes always darting back to the entrance to the ballroom.

The dancers slowly began to disappear from the floor until only Prince Sebastian and the lady he danced with remained.

They danced alone until King Hugo came to the edge of the balcony as to address the crowd in attendance. "*GOOD EVENING!*" his voice boomed. "*And welcome to this, the final night of the festival!*" The people cheered. "*We are nearing the conclusion of the ball, and as such, it is time for Prince Sebastian to name his choice! Tomorrow, we will bear witness to the marriage of our Crown Prince to our future Queen!*" The crowd clapped.

There was tension in the air, as though a thunderstorm was about to hit. "MY SON!" the King boomed. "Would you care to join me?" Prince Sebastian left the woman in the blue dress on the dance floor and climbed the stairs to the balcony to stand by his father. "My son," he repeated. "*I ask you, are you prepared to name your choice?*"

"I am, Father," Prince Sebastian responded. "*LADIES AND GENTLEMEN!*" he addressed the crowd. "As a King, it is my duty to ensure every choice I make is the best possible interests of our kingdom! As such, the selection of our Queen will impact us all!

"*Only* a maiden carrying the most meaningful qualities could be considered! She needs to be kind, but strong! She needs to be dignified but unafraid of hard work, showing great respect to the position she would be serving! She needs compassion to all within our kingdom and the dexterity to build and maintain our alliances with our neighbouring kingdoms!" Here, he turned and bowed to the visiting royals standing by his father.

"I am not seeking a *wife*, but a *partner*! Someone who will rule by my side as an effective leader of our kingdom! *I believe I have found that very woman! The Queen you all deserve!*"

Rufus heard a scuffle coming from down the end of the hallway and when he turned to look, he saw that in the entryway of the ballroom, an usher was *fighting* with a woman. She was wearing a long black gown with a corseted bodice. The dress was made entirely of peacock feathers though the green and blue eyes in each feather remained. They flared out at her shoulders to create a high off the shoulder sleeve.

Her golden hair flowed down her back. He had never seen a woman so beautiful. Correction, he had never seen this woman present herself so beautifully.

It was Asche.

The other people in the ballroom finally noticed the struggle as the usher, who Rufus finally recognised as Simon, finally lost his hold on the woman and she fell into the ballroom, grabbing hold of the staircase rail in front of her to stop herself from falling. All eyes were upon her, including Prince Sebastian's. "*LADIES AND GENTLEMEN, MAY I PRESENT TO YOU, YOUR FUTURE QUEEN!*" he announced grandly, holding out his arm towards Asche. "Mademoiselle, *please, what is your name?*"

Asche stood there at the top of the stairs, watching as every eye from the King to the guests stared back. Many of the women were glaring at her, including those of June, who looked outraged in her blue dress and the Contessa, who looked equally furious that the usher Simon had not been able to keep her contained as he had been instructed.

Asche made to walk down the stairs to join Prince Sebastian, to explain the situation, to tell him that she had no intention of marrying him or becoming Queen, but she was simply there to warn him of the deceit he had been about to face. Fate intervened; just as she took to the first step, the clock struck twelve; the first stroke of midnight.

The Fairy Godmother's words rang in her ears as loudly as though she were standing right beside her. *At the very last stroke of midnight, the spell will be broken and all will be as it was.* Panic gripped Asche, rattling her rib cage and taking all of the breath from her lungs. She immediately turned and fled back down the hallway, through the inner courtyard that had housed the banquets and into the entrance of the palace.

She had not been able to warn the Prince, but June and the Contessa's lies had surely become obvious in that she had *arrived*, proving June was not who she had presented herself to be. She had not been able to find Rufus explain why she was late, why she had almost not been able to attend, but surely she would be able to find him in town in the coming days explain what had happened. Perhaps he would forgive her?

She reached the top of the stairs that led down to the carriages. As she ran, she tripped ever so slightly. She ran on, despite the loss of one of her incredibly beautiful and intricate slippers, that upon pulling from the nook in the hazel tree, she found had turned from gold... into *glass.*

She climbed into the carriage, crying out even more desperately to Mr Toad than she had the previous night. "HURRY! WE *MUST* GET HOME QUICKLY! WE HAVEN'T A MOMENT TO WASTE!"

Mr Toad was well versed in the palace departures by now. He flipped the reins quickly and at once the mice horses exploded with speed, leading her down the streets of the city faster than she had ever thought possible. It seemed the palace guards had also learned. They were at the back of the carriage almost the entire way home.

When the third stroke of midnight struck, she had just managed to clear the palace gates. When the fifth stroke hit, she felt that the seat on which she was sitting seemed so much smaller than before. When the seventh stroke hit, she noticed that her dress was starting to turn back to the same simple grey it had been when she had first put it on. When the ninth stroke hit, she could tell through her little window that Mr Toad was looking significantly greener than he had when she first climbed into the carriage.

The eleventh stroke hit. The carriage was definitely smaller. She was struggling to fit her body inside. Her dress had completely disappeared and two extremely large lizards had crawled through the carriage windows and onto her lap for safety, shrinking every moment. The horses were almost half the size they were when they began their journey from the palace.

The twelfth stroke hit. Asche went flying into the bushes at the side of the road as the pumpkin rolled on down the street. She came to a bumpy stop at the foot of a tree, just as the palace guards rode past atop their chargers, destroying the pumpkin as they galloped over it.

She looked around her, first checking that she had broken no bones, then looking for the mice, toad and lizards who had been her companions these past days. She made to stand up and found that despite the magic having ended, she was still wearing a single glass slipper. She removed the slipper gently and held it in her hands.

The animals were all safe and well, though rather rattled from their experience. The mice and lizards she carried in her arms while Mr Toad sat on her shoulder. Then she steadily made her way back through the woodland to where her carriage would have been parked, had it still existed.

As she wandered back through the vegetable patch, she placed the lizards and the mice on the grass. Then she carried Mr Toad back to his stone in the fountain. "Thank you," she said to them, before looking to the sky, watching how brightly the stars glowed. "Thank you for everything," she whispered into the night for her Fairy Godmother... for Nixie.

She walked back through the kitchen door, much to the surprise of Arina and Heidi. "We have been waiting for you!" Heidi told her.

"Gerry has gone to fetch the Contessa," Arina continued. "We won' be overheard. Wha' happened Lass?"

"The Prince is aware that June is not who he thinks she is," Asche told them.

"Oh that *is* wonderful news!" Heidi said.

"Yes, it is," Asche said uncertainly. "But... no."

"Wha'ever is the matter Dear?" asked Arina.

Asche bit her lip, almost scared to admit it. "He... the Prince... He may have chosen me to be his bride."

Arina and Heidi stared at her dumbfounded for what felt like an age, before the both of them jumped out of their chairs and started squealing and screaming. It was enough to wake half of the neighbourhood.

"*Shhhh!* You *must* be quiet!" Asche said. "After what happened I am sure that the Contessa and my stepsisters will be home any minute and they cannot know that you know! I could not bear it if any harm came to you," she said.

"But this is *marvellous!*" Heidi said. "You can become Queen! Move to the palace! All of this will be ended for you?"

"But," Asche said sadly. "But I do not love him."

Heidi and Arina at first seemed confused, but then they nodded their heads. "The lad from yesterday?" Arina said softly.

Asche nodded. "I could not find him," she said, a tear rolling down her face. "And he works at the palace! The last thing he would have seen was the Prince proposing marriage to me! What if he never wants to see me again?"

"Love, I think we have far more to worry abou' than tha' tonight," Arina told her, placing an arm around her shoulders. "Le's just ge' you to bed shall we?"

"What will you do?" Asche asked.

"We are big girls," Heidi nodded. "We can take care of ourselves." Asche miserably climbed all three flights of stairs to her attic bedroom, finally lying down on her bed, where she began to cry.

17

Once again, she awoke to her door slamming. This time, however, it was her bedroom door. *"Do you have any idea what you've done?"* the Contessa Georgina snarled.

Asche rolled over and sat up in her bed. "I stopped you from deceiving the palace and forcing June onto the Prince," she declared.

Contessa Georgina looked mutinous. Asche had never seen her so angry. "How *dare* you!" she hissed savagely. "If you think that you are *ever* coming out of this room-"

"-I care not where I go, Stepmother," Asche told her bluntly. "I do not want the Prince, but I did not want him to be with someone he does not truly want to be with either."

"Well, it will not change much with you now, will it?" Georgina smile darkly. "The King has decreed that the wedding will go ahead at five o'clock this afternoon," she told her. "It appears a slipper was left behind? Whoever fits it will be the Prince's bride! And that *will* be June," she went on, hands on her hips.

"She will put on the slipper and marry him this afternoon. We will convince him that it is *you* that was the fraud, aimed to lead him away from his one true love. Who you are... nobody will know... and when they are married, no one will ever remember that *you* existed."

Even Asche was shocked by the great lengths the Contessa was going through to see June married to the Prince. She was horrified by the idea that she would trap a young man so viciously. Before she could say anything however, the Contessa left her room and locked the door behind her. Asche gazed back out the window, where she could still see the palace in the distance.

"Someone needs to help the Prince," she whispered to her empty bedroom.

♠

Prince Sebastian was in the palace with King Hugo and his brother and sister, the Prince Vladimir and the Princess Zarina. "I will do whatever it takes to find her," Prince Sebastian said.

"And we will do whatever it takes to help you, Brother!" Zarina said earnestly. "I am so sorry that you were finally able to connect with someone only to have her disappear in this way."

"Brother, are you sure she wants to marry you?" his brother Vladimir asked. "She has run each and every night of the festival," he explained when his father frowned. "Maybe she has no interest in becoming Queen?" he suggested.

"Then why come to the blasted festival at all?" King Hugo asked.

"The party?" Vladimir answered with a shrug of his shoulders. "A chance to see the palace?"

"What do we do?" Zarina asked. "How do we find her?"

"The royal guards are already taking the glass slipper to every maiden in the kingdom. The Viscount is leading them with the help of the Marquis," the King said. "They have assured me that they will find this maiden before the five o'clock deadline."

"I wish to be out there helping, Father!" Prince Sebastien exclaimed. "She is to be my *wife!* I want to be out there helping find her!"

"Your place is here, Son," King Hugo explained. "There is much to be done. If the wedding is to be at five o'clock, then all that is required is the maiden herself. You, however, have much to see to. Zarina, I presume you will do your best to assist?"

"Absolutely, Father."

"Then I shall leave you to it," King Hugo said, getting up to take his leave. Prince Vladimir watched his brother and sister leave. *Who in their right mind would go after someone who clearly did not want them?*

It was early afternoon when the Viscount arrived at the mansion of the Baron household with the Marquis and the slipper in tow. The guards lined up along the drive and formed an honour guard for the Viscount as he entered.

He was greeted at the front door by the Conte Digby Baron and his wife Contessa Georgina. "Welcome to our fair home Viscount Jarvis," Contessa Georgina bowed low.

"Thank you, Madame," Viscount Jarvis said graciously.

"Might we offer you some tea, Viscount?" Conte Baron offered. "I am sure that you have been on the move for a fair portion of the day."

"I most certainly have!" the Viscount answered. "And I would be most grateful for the hospitality."

"Arina! Heidi! Fetch the Viscount a tea tray!" Georgina called, clapping her hands. Heidi appeared almost instantly with the tea tray, Arina by her side carrying an identical tray laden with cakes and biscuits from Greta at the bakery.

"Well now, this is delightful!" the Viscount said. "But we mustn't tarry," he said officially. "Now, I must ask: Are there any maidens in the household?"

"Most certainly!" Contessa Georgina answered. "My daughters, the Lady June and Lady Charlotte." June and Charlotte were standing behind their mother. Georgina made a sweeping motion with her hand, directing the Viscount and Marquis' gaze to them with a flourish.

"Lady June... of the *Baron* household?" the Viscount repeated.

"Yes, Sir?" June answered, coming forward.

"You danced with Prince Sebastian last night, yes?"

"Yes, Sir, I did," June said, smiling. "We had a wonderful time. We had a wonderful time dancing each night," she went on. "But then that imposter showed up and the Prince pointed to her instead of me. I do hope that she is found and put away for such treachery! And I do hope the Prince sees that it was I all along with whom he was so infatuated." Throughout her speech, Digby watched his feet, his heart burning with shame.

"All in good time, my dear!" he said. "Marquis? The slipper, if you please?" The Marquis entered the foyer with a delicate glass slipper sitting atop a red and gold cushion. The glass was polished smooth and it shone in the sunlight.

"It is beautiful!" Charlotte said softly.

"It most certainly is, Mademoiselle," the Marquis agreed. "Who would like to go first?"

"I will, of course," June answered.

Heidi and Arina led the group into the conservatory, where they placed the tea trays on the round wooden table by the window. The Viscount took a seat as Arina poured him some tea. He began to sip as June took a seat on the cushioned sofa along the wall by the bookcases.

The Marquis knelt down beside her and gently lifted the glass slipper from the cushion. He then slid it straight onto her foot. Immediately it became clear that the slipper did not fit.

To the untrained eye, it simply looked as though the shoe was too small for her, but June could feel that something was physically stopping her from getting her entire foot into the slipper. She could not explain it, but a force prevented her from putting it on.

After almost a full minute of trying the Marquis said, "I am sorry, my dear. Perhaps we should move on?"

"*This is not possible!*" June snapped. "These are the impostor's slippers! Of *course* they are not going to fit me!"

"Well now, we have our orders Mademoiselle," the Viscount said. He took a bite of one of the biscuits from the tray. "Carry on! Who is next?"

"I am," Charlotte said, coming forward, taking a seat on the sofa. June shot daggers at her sister. She knew this was not Charlotte's choice; that each maiden in the kingdom would have to try on the slipper, but she could not prevent the obvious displeasure showing on her face.

Charlotte took the slipper from the Marquis and slid it onto her foot, but no matter how hard she tried she too could not put it on. First, a toe would not fit, then she could not get it over her heel.

After much less time than her sister she gave up and handed the glass slipper back to the Marquis. "I am sorry, Sir," she told him. "I hope you find her soon?"

"Thank you, my dear," the Viscount said graciously. "Now, unless there are any other young women in this household? Conte Baron, I believe that you have a daughter, do you not?"

"Oh, my husband's first wife died many, many years ago," Georgina cut in before Digby could respond.

"My-my daughter-" Digby began.

"-She has been away at finishing school for some time now," Georgina finished for him.

"I see," the Viscount said. "Well, if that is all?" The Viscount and the Marquis rose to head for the door.

Throughout this entire exchange, no one had noticed that through the kitchen door came two lizards, and no one had noticed when those lizards had slowly crept up the kitchen stairs, across the foyer floor, up to the banister railing that led up to the second storey, crawling along the windows all the way to the entrance to the attic. No one noticed when they climbed the long spiral staircase to the top of the tower and crawled through the keyhole of the attic door, unlocking it as they did so.

What everyone did notice, however, was when footsteps began pounding down the stairs, heading for the kitchen door. "*Mademoiselle!*" the Viscount exclaimed. "I was made to believe that there *were* no other maidens in this household?"

Asche was shocked. In her rush to escape her room, get into the city and find Rufus, find Nixie, find *answers*, she had not stopped to ensure that the Viscount and the King's men had arrived. She froze at the top of the stairs that lead down to the kitchen. "Sire?" she murmured, bowing slightly. "I-I am not a maiden of this household," she lied.

"No!" the Contessa Georgina agreed. "She is but a maid here! Off you go, Cinderella! Back to your work!"

"Cinderella..." the Viscount repeated. "May I have you join us in here please?"

Asche paused, uncertain, before she crossed the foyer into the conservatory, not meeting neither her stepmother nor her father's eyes. She continued to look at the floor as she took a seat in on the cushioned chair. She did not look up when the Marquis slid the glass slipper onto her foot and it fit perfectly. She did not clap along with the Viscount and the Marquis when they learned that their search was over. Asche knew her life was going to change. She would live in the palace. She was to be Queen! But... she would likely never see Rufus again.

Rufus was walking through the main street of the city. He was not going anywhere in particular, but eventually found himself out the front of *Oh Sew Nice!* Nixie's dressmaking shop.

He paused for a moment, before pushing the door open, a small tinkling sound disappearing into the back of the shop as he did made his way inside. "Nixie?" he called. "Are you there?"

"Rufus? Is that you?" Nixie called from the back of the shop, suddenly appearing through the back door. "Oh! It *is* you! Have you heard the news? Here for a new suit, are you?"

"What is it? What news?" he asked.

"The Prince has found his bride!"

Rufus deflated, his jaw dropping. "He has? He found the woman with the glass slippers?"

"*Yes!* I could not be happier for her! Come to the wedding with me this afternoon?" Nixie said, taking his arm.

"The wedding? This afternoon? I do not think I will be able to find it in me..."

"It will be at the event of the season! You simply *must* go!"

"I suppose I shall have to, given my role at the palace," Rufus sighed. "I cannot say I am looking forward to it, however..."

"Whatever would you not be looking forw-*Oh!* The maiden with the glass slippers!" she exclaimed. "The maiden you brought to me for her stepmother and stepsisters gowns!"

Rufus noted desolately. He could not bear the idea of watching Asche get married. She would make an incredible Queen and he could not possibly deny her such an opportunity. He loved her far too much for that.

"Your Highness! Your Highness! We have found her!" The guards came running into the entrance hall, where Prince Sebastian had been waiting for news, pacing back and forth. He had been through countless fittings and meetings with all manner of designers and decorators and cooks. He had had more than enough of it all, and so proceeded to make his way to the front of the palace to await the return of the Viscount and the Marquis.

"Are you sure? You have definitely found her?"

"We have, Sire!" one of the guards insisted. "She returns with the Viscount and the Marquis as we speak, from the Baron household, Sire!"

"The Baron household?" Not Lady June of the Baron household?"

"No, Sire. Her name is Cinderella."

Cinderella climbed down from the carriage and out into the sunlight. She had no idea when she woke up that morning that it was to be her wedding day. She knew that she was going into a life of luxury and privilege that she never thought was ever going to be possible for her and for that she should most definitely be grateful, for life was finally being kind to her. Surely this was her being given everything that she had ever dreamed of while she gazed at the palace from her attic bedroom window? Still... she could not forget about Rufus.

The Viscount carefully led her up the stairs, taking their time as she slowly climbed, ensuring that she had the time to collect herself before being presented to the Prince, for surely this was to be a momentous occasion for her and the Viscount and the Marquis truly did want her to enjoy it.

Cinderella stepped into the entrance hall, where she was immediately greeted by Prince Sebastian. "It *is* you! I knew I would find you!" she said excitedly.

"Hello, Your Highness," she bowed low. "I am glad that my stepsister was not able to deceive you with my stepmother's lies."

"Lies? How do you mean?"

"My stepmother specifically had June dress in the same colour that I had been wearing," Cinderella explained. "She was pretending to be me."

"The guards told me that you were a maid of the Baron household... but June is your stepsister?" he asked, confused.

"Yes, Sire," she answered. "I am both. My stepmother had me act as a maid after my mother died. I have been caring for my home and my family ever since."

"The Contessa Georgina LaBelle?" The Prince asked in almost a growl. "She treated you so?"

"My stepmother's life has been marred with much loss," Cinderella said almost protectively. "She has been through much, especially with the loss of her own husband before she came to marry my father. My father is a good man, but he was desperate for a loving home and family," she explained. "I forever served as a reminder of the life he had with my mother. I fear this lead the Contessa to behave towards me in a manner that she did not mean."

"You are quite forgiving," the Prince told her.

"When my mother died she told me that, above all, kindness and compassion are the most important qualities anyone can ever have, that placing further kindness into the world makes it brighter; more beautiful," Cinderella told him." I know that I will never suffer at her hands again and after having learned this lesson, I feel that no one else will either."

"You forgive so readily?" The Prince asked. "I could not possibly imagine doing so myself."

"No... I cannot imagine you would," Cinderella said simply.

The Prince looked at her curiously, as though unsure of how to respond. He chose to dismiss it entirely, instead bowing deeply before offering his arm. "Would you do me the honour of allowing me to introduce you to my father?"

"Of course, Your Highness," she bowed in return, before taking his arm. Prince Sebastien directed her through the entrance hall, but instead of moving into the hallway that led to the ballroom, he led her through a doorway to the left, which led to a series of rooms with long wide tables surrounded by high backed chairs with soft seats.

At the very end of this hallway was the throne room. It was a hall just as long, but not quite as wide as the ballroom, and all that it held was a long wide carpet that ran from the door all the way up to the raised wooden dais, whereupon sat two gilded thrones.

Currently only one of them was occupied. Cinderella was lead to the occupied throne, where King Hugo sat grinning from ear to ear like a little boy. "I have been most excited to meet you, Mademoiselle," he told her kindly.

"Thank you, Your Highness," she bowed again. She was already becoming irritated with how often she was needing to do so. "It is indeed an honour to meet you so personally."

"May I present to you, my daughter, the Princess Zarina and my youngest son, Prince Vladimir."

"It is wonderful to meet you," Cinderella replied, bowing again to Zarina before turning to Prince Vladimir. She straightened from her bow and froze in her place, unable to look away.

It was Rufus.

18

Asche was stunned. She could not believe what she was seeing. Rufus? The Prince? Why had he kept such a thing from her?

She did not know how to respond. Rufus took the initiative. He reached forward took her hand, kissed it gently and bowed. "It is a pleasure to meet you, My Lady. Welcome to our home," he said.

"Oh," Cinderella said softly. "Thank you, Sire."

"Well, we mustn't tarry!" King Hugo said with a clap of his hands. Seemingly out of nowhere two ladies in waiting appeared and took her by the elbows. "We have a wedding to prepare for!"

The rest of the afternoon passed in a blur. There were people fussing about her clothes and her hair and her face. When she was finally left alone to climb into her dress, she leapt back in shock as it began to sparkle and glow. When she could finally look at it directly again, it had changed. Instead of satin, it was now a peacock feather dress, a replica of the one she had worn the previous night, but instead of being black, it was pure white.

"Is this some sort of joke?" she whispered to herself as there was a knock on the door.

It was the Marquis with her glass slipper "I thought you might like to keep it with you, My Lady," he said. "As a token of luck."

"Lucky indeed," Cinderella muttered under her breath when he had departed, thinking to herself that it was the bad kind rather than the good.

Just as she was being led to the palace Chapel, there was a voice drifting in from outside. "Surely you would allow a man to walk his daughter down the aisle?"

"Father?" Asche said, turning towards the voice. "Father!"

"Asche, my darling!" Conte Digby Baron ran to her. He grasped her hands, looking into her eyes, before drawing her into her a hug, embracing her tightly. "Asche can you ever forgive me for all these years?" he asked quietly.

Asche thought of her mother. "Yes, Father, of course I can," she said to him. "I know what pain you are in; what the Contessa meant to you. I knew that you would not see yourself lose her as you did Mother," she told him.

"Would you allow me to see you to the Prince?" he asked, tears in his eyes.

"I would like that," she said. Her escort stepped aside as she took the hand of her father and he led her solemnly into the chapel, down the aisle to her Prince, the wedding processional playing slow and soft. It felt to Asche as though she were attending her own funeral rather than her wedding.

Every royal, dignitary and courtier had returned to the palace for the wedding of Cinderella Mariela Baron and the Crown Prince Sebastian Reginald Hubert Matthew Bishop the Seventh. She felt as though there were more eyes on her now than there had been at any of the previous balls. Thankfully, there was not to be another.

She delivered her vows quietly and solemnly, whereby she promised to have and to hold Prince Sebastian in sickness and in health, till death did they part. Cinderella almost choked on her words during this time, for through her veil she could still see Prince Vladimir on the other side of his brother, carefully avoiding her eyes.

Rufus... Her Rufus.

How is it that she would never again know the warm touch of his embrace, the gentle kisses of his lips on hers, the safety of his very presence?

Prince Sebastian delivered his vows and Cinderella was snapped out of her reverie when the priest announced that they were now man and wife. Her veil was drawn back and the Prince leaned forward and kissed her; not softly, not passion-ately; just a simple official kiss.

The crowd began to clap and sheer as Prince Sebastian took Cinderella's hand and led her back through the chapel, out the door and into the waiting sunshine of the palace courtyard, where she could see almost the entire city had lined up along the fences and palace boundaries in order to get the first look at their Crown Prince and his new Princess, if for only a few days, for the day after tomorrow there was to be a Coronation... Her Coronation and Asche the once maid and now Princess Cinderella... was to be Queen.

As Queen she would not be Asche. She had chosen to take the name that had been thrust upon her by her stepmother and stepsisters all those years ago, to go in line with the new life that had also been thrust upon her; that of a Royal Princess. Neither life she had chosen, so it seemed fitting that Cinderella was the name she should use for both.

The Prince led her into a carriage and they rode through the city, making lap after lap, waving from the windows to those who were unable to stand outside the palace and get the first glimpse of the couple. They lined the streets, cheering as the Prince and Princess drove past. When the last rays of the summer sun were finally disappearing below the horizon and the street lamplighters were coming with their torches, the Prince directed the carriage back to the palace.

"Are you excited?" Prince Sebastian asked her.

"I fear I am more nervous than anything else," she replied honestly.

"I can assure you that when it comes to being a royal there is quite the learning curve to it, my Princess," he told her. "I shall take the reins and lead you as much as I can, but there will be many years to come of you taking lessons to learn everything you need to know to be the best Queen possible for our people," he said. "You needn't fear that you must know everything all at once."

"That is most definitely something to be grateful for."

Prince Sebastian offered her his arm and she took it gently, before he led her up the main stairs of the palace, flanked by several guards. It was very different to any of her entrances from the King's festival from the previous three days.

The guards remained in the entrance Hall as the Prince took Cinderella up the grand staircase from the foyer to the second floor, where his personal quarters were. Her heart began to pound. She was not prepared for this; not this part.

As it turned out she had nothing to fear. The Prince passed his personal quarters, which Cinderella only knew whose they were due to Rufus'... *Vladimir's?* tour. He instead took her to the next door down. "These are your personal quarters, Cinderella," he told her. "I had the royal housekeepers ready them for you to ensure that you had your own space to get comfortable and settle in," he explained upon seeing the curious look on her face.

Cinderella released a breath that she hadn't realised she had been holding. That was certainly a relief... but also odd.

What man would not take up the opportunity to consummate his marriage on his wedding night?

She had spoken too soon. "I shall return after the meeting with my father and the other dignitaries," he told her. "It should not last long."

"You have a meeting? Tonight?" Cinderella asked.

"Royal duties never end," he sighed. He leaned forward and kissed her gently on the forehead. "You are free to do as you wish. You are home now. Feel free to explore as you will; go and get to know my sister. I am sure she is in the library and would appreciate the company. She has so little of it," Sebastian suggested.

"If these are Royal meetings," Cinderella began. "Then why would Princess Zarina not attend?"

"Well, despite how involved my sister may be in all matters of the state," Prince Sebastian said, a frown on his face. "Even she must understand that there are certain things that simply do not involve her."

Cinderella nodded understandingly. Prince Sebastian smiled. "You, my dear, get some rest; Explore! I can have the maids bring you something to eat if you like? Have you eaten?"

"Some tea would be lovely," Cinderella answered. She actually could not remember the last time that she ate. It must have been the tea Heidi and Arina had given her when Mr Toad and Mr Lizards released her from the cellar.

Oh, Mr Toad... Mr Lizards. I miss you so.

The Prince took his seat at the large wooden table on the right hand side of his father, King Hugo. To King Hugo's left was

Prince Vladimir, and there were many other royal courtiers besides, including the Viscount Jarvis and the Marquis.

"Thank you for joining us, gentlemen," the King greeted them. "We are here to discuss the transition of the kingdom from my rule, to the Crown Prince Sebastian's. The Coronation is scheduled for two days' time. How come the preparations, Jarvis?"

"We are right on schedule, Sire," he answered primly. He had a long scroll unrolled in front of him that held a monumental list of tasks that had to be done before Prince Sebastian could receive the crown, sceptre and cape that was his father's. "I have no fear that we may indeed miss your deadline," the Viscount finished.

"This is excellent news!" Prince Sebastian said. "I am ready! Is there anything that I can do to ensure everything runs smoothly?"

"Nothing more than see to it that our new Princess is ready to become Queen," the King said. "She is going through quite a change, based on what you told me regarding her home life." The King cleared his throat gruffly. "I have had the *former* Contessa's title stripped and both she and her daughters have been sent to the quarries," he announced.

Silence settled on the table. "It-it was very kind of you to step in on Cinderella's behalf, Father," Prince Sebastian told him. "From what she tells me they have mistreated her greatly."

"Do you not think she should have been given the opportunity to have a say in what happened to her family?" Prince Vladimir asked.

"I have spared her father, the Conte Baron," the King said. "And I would think that she would be most grateful for finding out that the people who mistreated her so have been punished appropriately. If, however, you are thinking it is too harsh then we can certainly sit down with the girl and ask what she would prefer."

"That certainly sounds reasonable Father," Prince Sebastian cut in. "Whoever they are, whatever they have done, she clearly still sees them as family. It would be remiss to not include her."

The King nodded thoughtfully. "For now, we must ready the two of you for Sebastian's Coronation."

Vladimir... *Rufus*, sat there unhappily, his heart hardening at the shocking turn of events. He had planned on marrying Asche himself and now she was married to his brother, to be coronated as his Queen in only two days. The pain became too much.

Vladimir rose from his chair and bowed deeply to his father. "Excuse me, Father, I am sure everything that needs doing will be done in a timely manner. Should you need anything of me please do not hesitate to call, however these past days have been quite exhausting and I would see that I get some rest to ensure that I am readily available for everything my brother needs in the coming days," he said with great politeness and propriety.

"Yes, my boy," the King answered. "But do not disappear entirely. We may be discussing your own marriage in the days to come!"

Vladimir paused as he made to leave, but turned back to Sebastian. "Congratulations, Brother."

Prince Sebastian watched him curiously, quickly getting up and following Vladimir out into the hallway. "Vladimir!"

He paused. "Is something wrong?"

"You seem out of sorts," Prince Sebastian said. "Is there anything on your mind?"

"It has just been a long week, and it is barely half over," Vladimir explained. "I am fine, I promise."

"So this isn't you disagreeing with my marrying or taking the throne?" Sebastian asked. "You appear less than welcoming to Cinderella."

"Cinderella," Vladimir laughed. "No; she will make a wonderful Queen, and *you* the perfect King. I am sure of it."

"Then I have your loyalty?"

"Always, Brother!" Vladimir insisted. "You simply have to accept that it is to be received from my bed as I sleep the night through for the first time in the last three days."

Sebastian nodded, not entirely convinced. "We shall talk tomorrow. I wish to share my plans for the kingdom with you! As my right hand man I need you on board with the direction we are taking the kingdom."

"Of course, Brother," Vladimir said. "I shall see you at breakfast."

Sebastian watched as his brother disappeared up the staircase, before returning to the meeting.

19

Cinderella sat upon her gilded four poster bed. Everything from the bedding, to the curtains, to her sitting furniture all had the same peacock blue colour trimmed in gold. It seemed she had created a bit of a stir with the colour and the housekeepers at the palace had insisted that everything she owned be that colour. "You shall be setting quite a trend, Princess!" one of her handmaidens had told her when they delivered her tea tray.

"I am not quite sure what that means," she had answered. "But thank you?"

The tea was gone, as were the biscuits that had sat with them on the tray. Cinderella was now sitting anxiously in a chaise, fearing exactly what would happen when the Prince returned from his meeting.

She could not take it anymore. Cinderella got up and made for her door, running out into the hallway and upon seeing it abandoned, made for the rooftop. She was breathing rather heavily by the time she arrived, having climbed three full flights of stairs in the heaviest gown she had ever worn.

She breathed in the night air gratefully, happy to not be within four walls. Just as she made for the edge of the parapets, she realised she wasn't alone.

"*Rufus?*"

"Asche? Is that you?"

The sun had gone down so he could not see that she nodded. He moved closer to her, to where the torchlight still fell. Their eyes met and time seemed to stand still.

Then they were running at each other. They did not stop until they collided, kissing each other as deeply and as fiercely as they never had before. "I am so sorry this happened," Asche said when she pulled away from him. "I never meant for this to happen!"

"Where were you?" Rufus asked. "I waited until sundown and you never arrived?"

"Georgina locked me in the cellar so I could not escape," Asche explained. "She had June dress like me to fool Prince Sebastian! I had to come and warn him but I never expected... this!"

"I know," Rufus told her. "I know."

"You! The *Prince!* Why did you keep this from me?"

"I am sorry," Rufus said genuinely. "I know I shouldn't have. I go by Rufus on the streets to avoid the attention that comes with being... Prince Vladimir."

Asche considered her own alter ego... Cinderella. "What do I do? I do not want to be Queen!" she told him.

"Unfortunately I have very little say in these matters," Rufus said quietly. "With the trouble my brother has been to in order to find a Queen... I do not think he will release you willingly." He held her close as Asche began to cry.

Far below Asche and Prince Vladimir, the meeting had ended. Prince Sebastian was making his way back to his quarters when he stopped at his Princess Cinderella's door. He frowned when he saw that she was not there. Even if she had gone looking throughout the palace, surely she would have returned by now.

He made for the library, thinking that perhaps she had joined his sister, Princess Zarina and they had lost track of time. The library however, appeared to be empty.

He returned to his quarters, angry. "Inform me the *moment* she returns!" he spat at a guard stationed outside their rooms, slamming his door behind him.

He stomped over to a woven tapestry that had been made when his mother died. Its image was him as a little boy, sitting on her lap as she read to him. He placed his hand over his mother's on the tapestry, before grabbing a fistful of the material and pulling it to the side, revealing a giant map of the continent pinned to the wall. Their kingdom had been outlined in blood red ink, one of the largest in the land. Directly to the north, a kingdom just as large as theirs was nestled between them and the sea.

"I promise you Mother," Prince Sebastian muttered under his breath. "I will not allow some scullery maid to prevent me from avenging you. She *will* fall in line. I *will* be coronated. Then, as King... Nowhorl will be *mine!*"

Dawn was just breaking when Cinderella finally returned to her rooms. As soon as she disappeared through the door the duty guard gave a swift knock on the Prince's. "Enter!" he called drowsily.

The guard entered, offering a bow as a naked woman with brown hair slid from the Prince's bed and disappeared into his private bathhouse. "Sire! The Princess has returned!"

Sebastian sat up straight in his bed. "Only now?"

"Yes Sire, she just arrived," the guard confirmed.

Prince Sebastian leapt out of bed, nodding to the guard, who bowed again, dismissed. He opened his wardrobe and dressed within minutes, before making for his bride's quarters.

He did not knock; simply turning the handle and slamming the door open, startling a half naked Cinderella as she stripped down out of her wedding gown. *"WHERE HAVE YOU BEEN ALL NIGHT?"*

"I-I am sorry, Sire!" she exclaimed, trying to cover herself. "I was exploring as you invited me to! I lost track of the hour!"

"Do not give me such blatant excuses!" he yelled, grabbing the dress from her hands and throwing it aside, leaving Cinderella just her hands to cover her chest. "YOU ARE TO BE QUEEN AND YOU DAMN WELL START ACTING LIKE IT!" he demanded. "The Kingdom expects better! *I demand better!*"

Cinderella cowered, shaking, unable to form a coherent sentence. Sebastian sneered. "Ensure you are on *time* for breakfast." He headed for the door.

Cinderella sat down on her bed, still shaking as the Prince left her room, flinching when the door slammed. She hoped that wherever he was... Rufus was alright.

♠

Breakfast was a staid affair. Zarina, King Hugo, Prince Sebastian, Prince Vladimir and herself all sat around a circular table as cooks and maids brought out plate after plate of food; cinnamoned toast, sausage, eggs and pastries of all types. Cinderella picked slowly at each plate, leaning more towards the tea than her food to settle her nerves after the events of the morning.

"So, what are your plans for today, my dear?" the King asked her conversationally.

"Me?" Cinderella asked. "The handmaidens have brought me many books. I believe they plan to have me studying most of the day."

"Very good," he nodded. "An excellent start! An educated Queen is an effective Queen!"

"And I shall stop in as well," Zarina offered. "Make sure the old fuddy duddies do not *bore* you to death before your Coronation," she laughed. "History is much more interesting the way *I* tell it," she winked. Cinderella smiled gratefully. "And whatever will *you* be doing, Brother dear?" she asked Sebastian.

"I am meeting with the courtiers today," he answered, taking a bite of his toast. "Informing them of the steps I plan on taking to further secure the needs of our kingdom once I am King."

"Intriguing!" she said. "I will have to attend in order to discover such secrets, shall I?"

"Oh I doubt you will hear anything to interest you, Zarina," he said, waving a hand. "Spend your time with Cinderella. Show her what she needs to know; you know what the priorities are. Make sure the handmaidens focus on *them* rather than wasting time on pointless frivolities such as the difference between off white and ivory!"

"Need I remind you, Brother, that my own marriage has been organised for within a year of your Coronation *explicitly* so I can advise you in these early days?" Zarina said, seemingly annoyed. "My role in the court is not to teach *manners*."

"Advisory role or not, Sister, you will still be expected to know your place!" Sebastian snapped. "When I require your advice, I shall seek it out!"

"That attitude is quite uncalled for, Sebastian," the King said.

"*Indeed!*" Zarina agreed. "I have trained my entire life devoted to the crown! *You* have been preparing for less than a week!" She got up. "Do not think for a *minute* that you have the ability to effectively rule without me or Father. You would flounder like fish on land!" She stormed out of the room.

"How *dare* she!" Sebastian exclaimed.

"You need to apologise," Prince Vladimir said immediately.

"What-?"

"-He said you need to apologise and I quite agree!" the King insisted.

"It is *she* who should apologise! Talking to the future King like that!" Sebastian said, flabbergasted that his father and brother had turned on him so.

"You think a crown makes you a King?" Vladimir asked.

"Zarina is right, Son," the King said flatly. "Her knowledge and skills will serve you as no others will and your lack of experience *needs* them. I will not leave the crown to someone who disregards the assistance of those with greater knowledge than they, and definitely not to someone who denies they require it entirely!"

Sebastian's face was stormy. Cinderella began to feel very nervous. He appeared to be sulking, but he took a deep breath and smiled. "You are right, Father, of course you are," he nodded. "I fear the stress of everything is getting to me. I shall find her and apologise immediately." He rose from his chair and bowed.

The King nodded, seemingly satisfied. He turned to Cinderella. "How was your first night in the palace, my Dear?" he asked her. "Hopefully far better than your first breakfast!"

"It was wonderful, Your Majesty," she smiled. "The people here are most kind," she said, glancing at Prince Vladimir.

"Quite so!" the King agreed, not noticing as he took another bite of his breakfast. "My wife was always of the opinion that those who serve us should be treated as family, for we would not have a happy and healthy one were it not for their efforts."

"I can most certainly respect that considering where I came from," Cinderella said. "The Queen was a wise woman."

"Yes," the King almost whispered, staring out the window as he was wont to do. "She most certainly was."

"And so my father was given a battlefield coronation, crowned as King then and there! He immediately withdrew his troops and sent messengers to every kingdom in the land, inviting them to meet with him; thus the Continental Alliance was born and the treaties we have with the other kingdoms are still in place to this day," Zarina finished her tale. "Our kingdom has known peace ever since."

"Then your father returned here and met your mother... and here you are!" Cinderella said.

"Here I am!" Zarina laughed, raising her arms above her. "Mother was one of the medics taking care of the returned soldiers. Father had every one of them housed here, where he could visit them *every single day*," Zarina told her. "Every recovery... every loss, he was there, and the day after the final deceased soldier was laid to rest and the final living soldier was sent home healthy and well, he and my mother wed.

"The both of them, for every day of their existence, devoted themselves to others. My father gives up the mantle of King because he feels his selfish desires for grandchildren and a growing family leads him to feel he can no longer serve the crown as he has before. *That* is the legacy you and Sebastian are stepping into," Zarina said seriously.

Cinderella nodded, deeply moved. "I understand. I promise to give everything I have to the kingdom. It may not be what Queen Roberta was capable of, but I will exhaust every last breath trying."

Zarina smiled. "I believe you, and I have no doubt you will. Being a Queen to a King is so vastly different from being a wife to a husband, but those roles remain intricately connected. My father has not been the same since my mother died, as a father as well as a King. It is part of the reason he abdicates; he believes the people deserve better," she explained.

"How did she die?" Cinderella asked. Zarina's eyes snapped up, her face suddenly hard. "I am sorry-I did not mean to intrude!"

Princess Zarina waved a hand at the handmaidens who were fussing with Cinderella's hair. "Leave us," she ordered. They had a moment's hesitation where they eyed each other, before bowing and leaving, closing the door quietly behind them.

After a moment Zarina sighed, looking down and playing with the embroidery on her dress. "What do you know about her death?"

"Only what the city was told," Cinderella said. "She fell ill. Healers were requested from all across the land. No one was able to help her... so she died."

Zarina nodded. "Yes, except something *could* have helped her," she admitted. "There was a ship of supplies in the harbour of a neighbouring kingdom. It had been left there since the war because no kingdom was allowed to lay claim to any spoils of war," Zarina explained quietly. "There was a shipment of medicines on it. Mother knew about it, she *told* them it would aid her... but the kingdom that housed the ship insisted they would not break the treaty for any reason.

"My father insists to this day that he understands why they made that choice, and often goes out of his way to prove his continuing goodwill, but he lives every day of his life knowing that it was possible for his wife to still be alive if only they had allowed the medicine to leave the ship," Zarina finished in a whisper.

"I am so sorry," Cinderella said, placing her hand gently over Zarina's. "Where was the ship?"

Zarina looked her in the eyes, almost fearful. "Nowhorl," she answered.

20

"We must ensure that no loss of life due to preventable means ever threatens our people again," Prince Sebastian was saying. "I propose that new treaties be drawn up between our kingdom and Nowhorl that releases any spoils of war to those in need. The spoils may not be sold or claimed by the kingdoms, but can be *donated* for charitable reasons."

"It is most definitely an admirable aim, Son," King Hugo said, agreeing with many of the courtiers as they nodded. "But Nowhorl have made their expectations quite clear. I feel you may have a hard time convincing them."

"You said so yourself, Father," Sebastian said. "Zarina is knowledgeable and skilled in this arena. I believe she could do it if given the opportunity."

"The King did say she had a gilded tongue," the King said thoughtfully. "Do you have a backup plan? Simply making a request to change a treaty has the potential to cause bad blood. You must tread carefully."

"I understand, Father," Sebastian said. "And you can rest assured I would never do anything I was not absolutely sure would provide a great benefit to our kingdom, and as it happens, I *do* have a backup plan should things go awry."

"You do?"

"Yes Father," Prince Sebastian was practically giddy. "A *marriage*."

"Marriage?" Viscount Jarvis repeated. "But Sire, you are already married?"

"I do not mean myself, Viscount."

"You are not suggesting Zarina marry into the Nowhorl family, are you?" the King asked. "Because you will not be able to stand against her if you try. Our terms were clear. She *will* be engaged within the year, but it must be *her* choice."

"I know that Father, and I think if the hole within our relationship with Nowhorl was rectified prior to her considerations for marriage, then we would have the possibility to strengthen our kingdom twofold," Prince Sebastian said.

"So you propose a marriage between us and Nowhorl, yet you see Zarina marrying someone from another kingdom?" the Viscount reiterated. "Then *who* would be participating in the marriage to Nowhorl?"

Prince Sebastian turned to his brother, Prince Vladimir, grinning.

"You cannot be serious?" Vladimir said flatly.

"Come now, Brother!" Sebastian said, clapping him on the shoulder. "You met Princess Willow. She is delightful and has Zarina's endorsement! They are still here for the Coronation. We should invite them to dine with us!"

"I have no interest in marrying the Princess of Nowhorl," Prince Vladimir told the room bluntly, getting to his feet. "And if you or Zarina will not have a partner forced upon you, neither will I!" Vladimir stormed out, ignoring the protesting mumbles of the seated courtiers.

"You cannot expect your brother to do what you and your sister would not," the King told Prince Sebastian. "If this treaty alteration is something you are seriously considering, I will back you, but you must find another way to maintain the relationship should negotiations fail."

"Yes Father," he nodded, staring after his brother. "I will not let you down."

♠

"He is actually suggesting now that *I* marry the Princess of Nowhorl!" Rufus was telling Asche. They were back up on the roof of the palace. Asche's lessons had ended for the day and Rufus had been up there since he had stormed out of the meeting.

The Coronation was the next day. Asche had resigned herself to the idea of becoming Queen. After hearing what Princess Zarina had to say about how King Hugo and Queen Roberta had devoted themselves to their people first and everyone else after, Asche believed that she could most definitely separate Cinderella the Queen from Asche the maid. She had already committed herself at this point; she was going to make sure that commitment was felt across the entire kingdom.

He had told her about what had become of her stepmother and stepsisters. That sort of severe punishment for crime was something she intended to broach when she was Queen. "What will that mean for the kingdom? What does the marriage provide?"

"Sebastian believes it will push Nowhorl to alter the war treaty," he said. "It will mean all spoils of war can be moved across kingdom borders as long as they are going to those in need," he scoffed. "It is *madness!*"

Asche looked at her hands in her lap. "Zarina told me about what happened... with you mother," she admitted.

Rufus looked pained. "He behaves as though this will bring her back," he whispered. "And that both my marriage and Zarina's will cement relations with potentially lost allies that will guarantee a peaceful reign for him. It is incredibly naïve."

"But this marriage," Asche said delicately. "It has the potential to guarantee many years of peace, does it not?"

"Asche, what are you saying?" he said. "You think I *should* marry the Princess of Nowhorl?"

"I think you should do whatever is necessary to take care of the people of this kingdom," Asche replied. "And if that means making certain sacrifices of happiness to ensure their health and safety... that is something we should be willing to do. What will you do if you do *not* marry the Princess of Nowhorl?"

"I do not know!" Rufus exclaimed.

"Would you simply find someone else to marry?"

Rufus froze. He held her face in his hands as tears fell from her eyes. "I could never."

"Whatever we do, the kingdom comes first," she whispered, holding her forehead to his. "Even if that means I get Coronated, and you marry Willow. Even if it means you and I will never be..."

Rufus nodded, not moving his hands from her face. "Yes."

♠

"MAY I PRESENT TO YOU YOUR *KING*, HIS ROYAL MAJESTY KING SEBASTIAN REGINALD HUBERT MATTHEW BISHOP THE SEVENTH, AND YOUR QUEEN, HER ROYAL MAJESTY *QUEEN CINDERELLA!*"

Queen Cinderella stood with the now King Sebastian at the top of the stairs overlooking the palace entrance. It seemed as though every citizen of the kingdom had travelled to the city for the coronation and every one of them stood before her. Everywhere she looked were masses of bodies, so tightly packed that she could not make out any distinct faces.

The remainder of the day was filled with a parade, a banquet and a personal introductory meeting with the royal families of every kingdom in the land, followed by a dinner. At its conclusion, King Sebastian and Queen Cinderella were introduced to their personal staff.

"My mother and father had their right hands as their most loyal and trusted friends for all the years they served with them," Prince Sebastian told her. "I would see that my right hand be Vladimir, for none could I trust more than my own brother." Vladimir gave a stiff nod.

"I agree," Cinderella said. "And given I have few close friendships, I could not consider anyone more suitable for the role as my right hand than Zarina."

Zarina gave a mock bow but laughed. "I would be delighted! Finally, *someone* around here recognises my genius!"

King Hugo chuckled. "I am gladdened that you should all take on the responsibility of the kingdom together; a problem shared is a problem halved as they say!"

"Well, Your Highness, I hope to never consider this kingdom a problem," Cinderella said. "But the problems *of* the kingdom shall most certainly be rectified faster if we work together." She then changed tact. "To that end, I would like to propose that a new structure for crime and punishment be developed."

"Oh?" Sebastian said curiously. "To what end?"

"I greatly appreciate how rapidly the royal family leapt to my defence upon learning of the mistreatment from my family," Cinderella began. "However the quarries offer very little by means of genuine rehabilitation for those sent to them."

"What would you suggest?" Zarina asked interestedly.

"There is much meaningful work needed to be done around the city," Cinderella said. "Streets requiring pavement, walls to be rebuilt, parks to be cleaned! The people at the quarry could be taught to care for their kingdom as we do, learning that there is far more to their lives within it than the crimes they have committed," she finished.

"What an intriguing idea," Hugo said, running his hands along his beard.

"I would like to start with my stepmother and stepsisters," Cinderella said to the royal secretary, who sat by the door making notes of the first official meeting of the palace staff. "I want them brought to me immediately."

"Yes, Your Majesty!"

21

“**I**s there any news on the meeting with the King of Nowhorl?” Prince Vladimir was asking his brother, the now King Sebastian. Vladimir was sitting in the opposite seat at the meeting table, where once Sebastian had sat. The former King Hugo was sitting in his old seat, while his brother now sat at the head of the table.

“Yes, in fact. Viscount Jarvis?” Sebastian called down the table.

“Yes, Your Majesty!” Jarvis confirmed. “Ten o’clock tomorrow morning, right after breakfast!”

“That is good,” Vladimir nodded.

“Why do you ask, Brother? You have made your feelings made clear on the matter.”

“This is true... however after much consideration I feel I may have had a change of heart.” It broke his heart to say, but Asche was right. It was the duty of the royal family to secure its welfare, regardless of whatever personal sacrifices need be made.

Sebastian leaned back, his eyes wider than before. “What has brought about such change in the span of a day?”

“You were coronated twelve hours ago Brother and yet here we sit, with much changed already.” Vladimir pointed out. “Do you not believe me capable of the same?”

“On the contrary! What I mean to say is that... you seemed rather *adamant* in your decision.”

Vladimir inhaled and exhaled slowly, forcing composure. “I was reminded that I am a member of the royal family... and as such, certain sacrifices are necessary in order to do what is right for the kingdom."

Hugo smiled. "I am proud of you, Boy," he said huskily. "Damn good of you."

"Quite!" King Sebastian exclaimed. "Brother, this is *marvellous!* You *are* doing the right thing, and I am sure when all is said and done you will be as happy in your marriage as I am in mine.

"Thank you for joining us this evening gentlemen. We shall reconvene tomorrow night and I will update you on the results of the meeting with the King of Nowhorl! Have a lovely evening." Sebastian stood up, collecting the papers in front of him as the courtiers slowly left. "Brother! Join me on the walk back to our quarters?"

"Of course, Brother." They climbed the staircase outside the meeting room to the second floor, making their way through the galleries to the hall of His Royal Highnesses royal quarters.

"Vladimir I cannot begin to thank you for this," Sebastian began. "I have lost sleep for many nights wondering after this treaty and how to guarantee losses such as Mothers *never* occur again." His voice suddenly sounded poisonous.

"I am doing my duty Sebastian... as Father has done, as Mother did in her own time."

"AS MOTHER WOULD *STILL BE* IF ONLY NOWHORL HAD ALLOWED IT!" Sebastian exploded.

"Brother! *Calm* yourself!" Vladimir exclaimed.

"Whatever is the matter?" a small voice asked. Cinderella. They had reached monstrous gilded doors that led to the King and Queen's chambers. Three armed guards stood on either side. Vladimir looked down, not able to look at her.

Sebastian planted a smile on his face. "Nothing at all, my Queen!" he called. "We shall speak at breakfast, yes?" he asked Rufus.

"Yes, Brother," Vladimir answered, before disappearing down the hall, leaving Cinderella and Sebastian standing alone.

"How was the meeting, my King?" Cinderella asked.

"Wonderful!" he answered brightly, walking into the chambers. "Vladimir has agreed to marry the Princess of Nowhorl!" He took of his coat jacket and turned to place it over a chair. "And I am one step closer..."

"Closer?"

Sebastian paused. "Think nothing of it, my dear!" he took her shoulders in his hands. "Tell me, what happened with your stepmother?"

"Nothing at all yet," Cinderella shrugged. "They have been returned from the quarries. I shall meet with them tomorrow."

"You have taken to the mantle of Queen as a fish to water! Is this not better than romping about the palace all hours of the night?" Sebastian asked.

"Quite, Your Majesty," Cinderella breathed, remembering the hatred on his face when he had come into her room the previous morning. "It-it is my duty to ensure the kingdom is taken care of."

Sebastian regarded her curiously. "You know... Vladimir said much the same... Have you two been speaking?"

"Not often," Cinderella lied. "But I cannot help but share Zarina's views on royal behaviour. She is quite passionate," she went on nervously. "It is hard to keep oneself from getting swept up."

"Ah, Zarina..." Sebastian sighed. "Well, if her high standards have put Vladimir on a plan that gets us one step closer to Nowhorl then she will be worth *every* headache!" he declared, removing his gloves.

"Now, we still have a matter to settle, do we not?" he smirked, holding out his hand. "Join me in my room."

"I do not think that wise, Sire," she answered quickly, backing away and shaking her head.

He frowned. "What on earth are you talking about?" he snapped. "It is a rather important part in a marriage, is it not?"

"It certainly is," Cinderella nodded. "But you must maintain your focus on Nowhorl right now."

"I think I can misplace my focus for a single night!" Sebastian said.

"Maybe you can," she agreed. "But I am not going anywhere and until you have made a position for yourself amongst the other kingdoms, there is simply no need for an heir," she explained. "Keep your focus on Nowhorl. I *know* how important this treaty is to you!" Sebastian looked away. Cinderella took his hand. "Zarina told me about what happened to your mother..." It was a low trick, playing on the King's pain over the loss of his mother, but she was willing to do just about anything to not find herself in his bed.

"So you expect to walk the halls as Queen while my needs go unmet?"

At this Cinderella laughed, a high genuine laugh. "*Unmet?* Your Majesty, you have every need you could possibly desire met at the hands, lips and hips of any maiden you fancy!"

A look of shock and embarrassment crossed the King's face. "How-?"

"-I heard you just last night Sire," she sighed. "I was in my room at a *respectable* hour, as you expected and it was *you* who returned long after midnight accompanied by far more voices than one!"

Sebastian stared in disbelief. "And... and you do not seem angry at all."

"You selected me for no other reason than that you *had* to select someone to be Queen," Cinderella said bluntly. "And I am committed to doing that role its due diligence, but I expect the same from you. Your role as King should be your number one priority-"

"-It *is* my number one priority!" Sebastian exclaimed.

Cinderella took a deep breath, regaining her patience. It felt as though she were explaining to a toddler why he could not eat mud. "It comes before everything, Sebastian," she said softly. "Including whatever relationship you and I share.

"You meet your needs however you see fit, but until you are situated and have made a name for yourself as *King* there is no need for an heir and until there *is*, your needs should be met elsewhere. You and I have far more important things to be doing as King and Queen than as husband and wife."

His frown had turned into a look of wonder. "You would place my ambitions as King over my father's ambitions of becoming a grandfather?"

"He passed the crown to you because he felt his desires were selfish and the kingdom deserved better," Cinderella reminded him. "He would make the same committed decision if he were in our shoes. As much as he dislikes having to wait, I feel he would greatly respect our devotion to the kingdom."

Sebastian looked up. "You are *remarkable* do you know that?"

"I am beginning to suspect," she smiled back, relief flooding her.

"Guard!" he yelled.

"Sir?"

"Go and fetch Freja, will you?"

The guard looked from Sebastian to Cinderella, as though unsure if it were a trick or a test. He finally bowed. "Yes, Your Majesty!"

"Have a delightful evening, my Queen!" he kissed Cinderella on the cheek and disappeared into his bedchamber.

Cinderella immediately got up and almost ran out the main doors. "I most certainly shall!" she whispered, closing them behind her.

Rufus was waiting for her on the roof. "How did you manage *again* to get away?" he asked, incredulous.

"This time I simply told him that until he wanted an heir there was no need and that he should simply live his life as he had before; chasing the handmaidens."

Rufus laughed. "What did he say?"

"He was shocked that a wife would allow such a thing, but I told him that being an exemplary King was more important than being an exemplary husband and I do not believe he has any interest in an heir at the moment," Asche told him. "He is behaving quite strangely. This meeting with the King of Nowhorl has much of his focus. He keeps saying he needs to get *close* to them," she said as they looked out over the hunting forest.

"I have noticed the same," Rufus said. "When you arrived in the hallway this evening... he had been ranting about how they were responsible for what happened to Mother. He seemed angry with them. It makes very little sense that he would want such a close relationship with a kingdom he feels has wronged us so."

Asche considered everything she had seen; everything Sebastian had said, what Zarina had told her about Queen Roberta, and what Rufus was now saying about his behaviour. "Rufus," she said quietly. He turned away from the forest to look at her. "What if... what if he does not mean to forge a greater bond with Nowhorl at all?"

"What are you suggesting?

"What if the marriage is simply... a ploy? A red herring? One step in a plan to strike at Nowhorl in some way?"

Rufus placed his chin on his hands, the magnitude of what she had said settling on him.

22

"Thank you so taking the time to join us today, King Linas, Queen Harriet, Princess Willow," Zarina greeted the royal family of Nowhorl as they took their seats at the long meeting table.

She sat across from Princess Willow, Vladimir and Hugo sitting either side of her. At the head of the table sat King Sebastian, King Linas sitting to his left, Cinderella to his right.

"We want nothing more than our kingdoms to coexist peacefully," Queen Harriet said. "And Viscount Jarvis insisted this matter was quite urgent?"

"I would think that it is, yes," Sebastian said lightly. "I believe we may have a way to bond our kingdoms far beyond friendship. I know that we have our treaty from the war and my family and yourself, King Linas, will forever be friends, however I believe we can do better."

"So we heard!" King Linas said, indicating to Zarina. "This one had us convinced with her pretty words, did she not Harriet? Willow?"

"She most certainly did, Father," Willow agreed, smiling widely.

"It is wonderful to know our kingdoms' relationship stands on such solid ground," Queen Harriet said. "To offer such effort and resources was very moving."

"I am not referring to the bargain you struck with my father and sister," Sebastian announced. "I am suggesting a new agreement entirely."

"And what would that be?" King Linas asked suspiciously.

"I am suggesting... an engagement, between Prince Vladimir and Princess Willow."

Several things happened at once. Zarina clapped her hand over her mouth, Queen Harriet gasped and placed a hand over the gold necklace at her throat, Cinderella felt herself go pale, Willow's jaw fell open and King Linas slammed his hand down on the table.

"When was this decided?" Zarina asked breathlessly.

She was drowned out completely by King Linas. "WE MUST TOAST TO THIS MOMENTOUS OCCASION!" he roared, getting up, practically skipping around the table to launch himself into a vicious embrace with Hugo, who laughed and pretended to fight him off. "THIS IS A FINE DAY FOR CELEBRATION!"

"Father, do I not get a say in this?" Princess Willow asked, near tears.

"Princess Willow, if I may?" Vladimir cut in. "Could we talk for just a moment?"

Fear and confusion on her face, she looked at Vladimir's offered hand and took it, allowing him to lead her out of the meeting room as she gazed back over her shoulder mournfully.

"She will come round to the idea," King Linas said dismissively, returning to his seat. "Now, let us see to these plans!" he boomed merrily. "We are all here; may as well have the wedding immediately! What a way to bring in your Kingship than with a bonding of our kingdoms that will last a lifetime!"

"There is much to discuss before we get to the wedding plans, Your Majesty," Sebastian insisted. "If I may?"

"Of course! What is your proposal?" The King seemed blissfully unaware of any malfeasance.

"Almost thirty years ago you and my father, along with the other Kings of this land developed the Continental Alliance by signing the Kingdoms War Treaty," he began.

"Yes? And?"

"I would ask that amendments be made to that treaty." Queen Harriet glanced at her husband, who had turned an odd shade of purple. "I believe that by adding a proviso to the treaty that allows any spoils of war to be donated to those in need, then we can ensure that no resources are left to waste... and no lives are lost unnecessarily due to the unavailability of such resources," Sebastian finished, interlocking his finger on the table in front of him. "The amendment would help many, and is that not what we all want?"

"You have brought us here under false pretences," Queen Harriet said quietly. "Hugo, how could you allow this?"

"I believe my son's request is a reasonable one," Hugo said. "He could have been more honest about his intentions, but his aims are honourable." He turned to King Linas. "Surely you would agree that sending resources to the needy is a charitable resolution to the issue of spoils of war?"

"THIS HAS NOTHING TO DO WITH CHARITY AND YOU DAMN WELL KNOW IT!" King Linas roared, turning back to Sebastian. "This is about your mother!"

"I would not see innocent lives like hers lost when it could be prevented," Sebastian growled, getting to his feet. "Kindly sit down."

"I will not! And I will not amend the treaty!"

"Let me make myself *clear*," Sebastian said in a dangerously low voice. "No amendment... *no marriage.*"

King Linas spat and sputtered with rage. "The *nerve!*" Queen Harriet exclaimed. "To bring us here under the guise of building bridges between our kingdoms, only to blindside us in this manner? The treaty has stood for decades. It guarantees fairness across the entire continent!" she continued. "We could not alter the treaty even if we wanted to! That could only be done with another meeting with the Heads of State and that has not been done since the Continental Alliance was first founded."

"Ah, but I *have* met with the other Heads of State," Sebastian declared. "They were all here for the King's festival, and each agreed to my recommendation. They will not be pleased that you are the holdout when this amendment could be a benefit to us all," he said lightly, disregarding their anger.

"*You met with the other Heads of State behind our backs?*" King Linas raged. "*HUGO!* What have you to say about this?"

Hugo appeared stunned by Sebastian's revelation. It seemed that this was news to him just as it was to the Nowhorl royals. "I do not know what to say, Linas," he said. "I would never dream of hiding such a thing from you; surely you know that? And I most certainly would not deliver the offer of marriage as an ultimatum!" He directed the last line to Sebastian, red in the face. "I would never have believed this of you if I had not witnessed it myself."

Cinderella watched on, horrified. This had been Sebastian's plan all along. Present the offer of marriage and include the treaty amendment as a term of the contract *knowing* they could not accept without the other Heads of State. By meeting with them without Nowhorl, Sebastian had created an alliance against them... one that Nowhorl could not possibly hope to stand against. Sebastian had found a way to get revenge for his Mother, no matter the cost... and he had used the crown to do it.

♠

Out in the hallway, Princess Willow had flown into a panic the second they had left the room. It had lasted for almost a full minute before Vladimir had been able to calm her.

"Princess, *please*-!"

"-I CANNOT POSSIBLY MARRY YOU, VLADIMIR-!"

"-Princess, if you just allow me to explain-!"

"-It is *not* that you are not wonderful, because I am sure you are-!"

"-You must listen to me-!"

"-*I am in love with someone else*-!"

"-SO AM I!"

Silence.

Willow stared at him for an uncomfortably long time, slowly catching her breath. "What?" she said flatly.

"I have no interest in marrying you any more than you do me," Vladimir insisted, his hands out.

"Then... then why-?"

"-Because my brother is actively trying to alienate your kingdom and he is being quite smart about it," Vladimir told her. "I agreed to do this so I could get close enough to figure out what his plan is."

"What are you talking about? He is proposing a marriage between us to *bond* the kingdoms! Why ever would he do that if he was trying to cut us off from the others?" Willow asked.

"I agree; it appears to make no sense, but see... he does not *want* the marriage to go ahead, at least, not on your father's terms. He wants revenge for what happened to our mother-"

"-Queen Roberta? What does her death have to do with this?"

"The ship in the Nowhorl harbour?" Vladimir said. "That held the cargo from the war?"

"Yes, what about it?" Willow seemed more confused that when they began.

"You do not know? It held a vital medicine that could potentially have saved my mother. Your father refused to allow it to cross his borders into our kingdom because it violated the Kingdoms War Treaty," Vladimir explained. "Sebastian blames him for our mother's death. He has requested an amendment to that treaty with your marriage to me as a means of buttering him up… so he has cause to turn the other kingdoms against yours when they refuse."

"Why would they refuse?"

"Why did they when the request was made while my mother still lived?" Vladimir retorted. "One way or another my brother will spin whatever happens in that meeting in such a way as to sour their relationship with every other kingdom in the Continental Alliance and destabilise the peace our parents worked so hard to cultivate if we do not do something to stop him."

Willow looked to the doors of the meeting room, fear on her face. Then they slammed open and the King and Queen of Nowhorl came storming out. *"WILLOW, WE ARE LEAVING!"* King Linas bellowed. *"IMMEDIATELY!"*

"Wait! Please!" Zarina cried out, following them into the hallway.

"NO MORE FROM YOU!" King Linas demanded. *"I'LL NOT HEAR ANOTHER WORD FROM THAT SERPENT TONGUE!"*

"Is this really how you choose to respond, despite the hospitality we have shown you?" Sebastian asked coolly, joining them in the hall.

"Hospitality?" King Linas spat. "This entire trip have been nothing but a waste of time and energy! And for *you*, a young upstart King with no experience and even less sense to have disrespected my family in such a manner? *The Alliance will hear of this!*"

"No... I do not think they will," Sebastian sighed. *"Guards!"*

Within seconds the royal family of Nowhorl were surrounded. "Sebastian! What are you doing?" Zarina said, terrified.

"Securing the safety of the kingdom and making sure what happens to Mother never happens again... even if that means taking Nowhorl completely," Sebastian said icily. "Take them to the dungeons."

23

"**W**hat on earth do you think you are doing?" Zarina screeched over and over as the guards hauled the Nowhorl royals away.

"Son there is *no* coming back from this!" Hugo yelled. "You have no idea what you have done!"

"I know exactly what I have done Father!" he hissed venomously. "I have done what *you* never could! I am doing what *you* failed to! I am doing right by Mother so she can rest knowing the people responsible for her death are finally paying for it!"

"*THAT IS ENOUGH!*" Hugo roared. "THIS IS OVER!" He puffed and panted in his outrage. "I am retaking the crown. It was clearly a mistake to abdicate. You are not ready... and you never will be."

"It is too late, Father," Sebastian said, eyebrow raised. "You are *nothing* to this kingdom anymore... GUARDS! Take him away too."

"*NO!*" Zarina screamed hysterically. "Sebastian! See reason!"

"What do you charge me with?" Hugo growled as guards took his arms, highly uncomfortable but unwilling to question a direct order from their King.

"Sedition."

"Sebastian STOP!" Zarina sobbed.

"ENOUGH OR YOU ARE NEXT!" Zarina fell silent, stepping back. Cinderella took her hand, squeezing it gently, as silent tears fell down Zarina's face. "And what of you, my Queen?" he said coldly. "Are you with me... or with *them?*"

Cinderella gave Zarina's hands a final squeeze, before letting go and moving forward. "I promise you, my King, there is *nothing* I will not do secure this kingdom and deliver to our people *exactly* what they deserve," she told him, unflinching. "I said that my role as Queen would come before nothing else and I meant it."

Sebastian's face softened slightly and he nodded. "You do mean it, don't you?"

"I do. Now tell us, what do you need?"

"What do I need?" he repeated.

"Yes, Brother," Vladimir came forward. "The Nowhorls are contained, Father will be secured; what comes next?"

Cinderella had not lied when she said she would do anything to protect the kingdom, but it had officially become in the best interests of the people to return Hugo to the throne. Vladimir had caught on quickly. *He is trying to get Sebastian's plan!*

"You are with me Brother?" Sebastian asked softly.

"You are not only my Brother, but my King, and I agree with Cinderella. The kingdom comes first."

"YOU ARE ALL INSANE!" Zarina screamed.

"No Zarina, you simply do not understand all that has occurred," Cinderella told her gently. She nodded slowly, before turning back to Sebastian. "I will return her to her quarters and keep her there until you two come for us."

"Yes... Yes, do that," Sebastian said. "I will have the guards escort you." He clicked his fingers. "Come, Brother. I must call a war council with the courtiers and other Heads of State... if we are to obtain Nowhorl for ourselves."

Vladimir gave Cinderella a knowing look before he turned to follow Sebastian. She took Zarina's hand again and pulled her down the hallway, the guards at their sides.

"I cannot believe you are going along with this *madness!*" Zarina snapped. "I thought you had sen-*ow!*"

Cinderella had dug her nails into Zarina's hand. "Unless you want to join your Father and the Nowhorls in the dungeons, I would *hold your tongue!*" She saw the guards were peering at them, watching closely. "There is much you do not understand. Once I enlighten you, all will become *clear*," she finished forcefully.

The guards stayed on either side of Zarina's door as they entered. Cinderella made a point of stopping before she followed Zarina in. "Gentlemen I have a meeting with my stepmother and stepsisters at noon. Be sure to inform me when the time draws near; I mustn't miss it!"

"Yes, Your Majesty!" They bowed.

Cinderella gracefully crossed the threshold and gently closed the door... before she ran at Zarina quickly covered her mouth just as she appeared to be readying herself to restart her tirade. "You *must* be quiet, Zarina! We cannot stop Sebastian with you locked away too."

Zarina immediately ceased her struggling. Cinderella moved her hand. "You lied?"

"No, I did *not*," she insisted. "I am *Queen*, and I *will* protect my people and serve my kingdom as they deserve... even if that means I must betray my King to do it. I promised Sebastian that the kingdom would come before everything, including us, and I meant that."

Tears once again sprang to Zarina's eyes. "We have to get them out of the dungeons."

"We will not let anything happen to your Father; I promise."

Zarina turned and surveyed the city through her bedroom window, her auburn hair glinting in the sunlight. "My father," she whispered softly.

♠

Shouts and yells were echoing all around the throne room. Every courtier and foreign royal had questions and demands; opinions on what the kingdom's next move was to be.

"I UNDERSTAND THIS HAS COME AS A GREAT SHOCK!" Sebastian called to the gathered nobles. The room steadily quietened to low muttering. "But the decisions to be made falls on my kingdom to rectify, as it has occurred on our soil! I *promise* you, I will not allow Nowhorl or my father to damage the Alliance! We have stayed strong all these years and we can remain so if we *stand together!*

"The amendment to the treaty will see *no* resources wasted, and with our kingdom in control of Nowhorl... *until* of course the Alliance decides what is to come of the nation, the prosperity we have known will continue for many years to come!" There was some clapping.

"I cannot possibly believe King Hugo would ever be traitorous!" a voice yelled from the crowd. Viscount Jarvis came forward to address the room. "I was on the battlefield when he was named our King, after the loss of his father and brother! Never has he led our fair kingdom astray! That is... not until the day he passed the crown to *you!*" he pointed directly at Sebastian. "*I stand with King Hugo*... ALL HAIL KING HUGO!" he cried.

"GUARDS!" Sebastian yelled angrily. "*Take him away!*" The Viscount continued screaming all the way out of the throne room. "PREPARE YOURSELVES FOR A NEW AGE, KINGS AND QUEENS, LORD AND LADIES!" Sebastian took his time settling himself into what was once his father's throne. "The traitors... die at sundown."

"He is going to *execute* Father?" Zarina squeaked, hiding her face with her hands.

"No," Vladimir assured her. "I promise I will not let that happen."

"What can we do to stop him?"

"I need to get back to Sebastian," he said. "You and Asche need to find a way to get down to the dungeons and get Father and the Nowhorls *out!* Where is she?"

"Asche?"

"Uh... Cinderella," Vladimir corrected himself. "Cinderella, where is she?"

Zarina eyed him suspiciously. "You have a pet name for our brother's *wife*? Anything to tell me Vlad?"

"Overly concerned about the Nowhorls, Sister. Anything to tell *me*?" he replied mockingly.

Zarina looked away, blushing. "She is with her stepmother and stepsisters."

The former Contessa stood before her, dirty and dishevelled, June and Charlotte standing on either side of her. Two guards stood at the door of the room, watching attentively.

"Do you know why you are here?" Cinderella asked.

"No," Georgina answered bluntly. "Unless you have decided the quarries were not enough and have ordered our execution?"

"Mother!" Charlotte hissed softly.

"Oh, now *you* have turned against me too?"

"That is enough!" Cinderella demanded. The room fell silent. Irritable as Georgina LaBelle was, she was not about to refuse the Queen. "I have brought you here for one reason and I must deliver it readily as I have other matters of state that take precedence over petty family matters."

Georgina suddenly looked interested. "Matters of state, you say?"

"Indeed," Cinderella said. "I have brought you here because as Queen, I have put an end to all forms of menial punishment. The expectation henceforth is that you provide much needed assistance to the kingdom in a meaningful way."

"We will not be returned to the quarries?" June asked, eyes wide.

"No."

June began to cry. "Thank you, Asche! I am so sorry for everything we put you through!" She dropped to her knees. "I never wanted to be this way! I swear I will do better!"

"My name is Cinderella," she responded. "Calm yourself, Sister," she instructed, raising a hand. "You and Charlotte will remain with me here, in the palace. You are to report to the Head Housekeeper immediately. She will see to it that you are bathed and given a bed. Tomorrow you will start work."

June scrambled to her feet and she and Charlotte were escorted from the hall by a guard. Georgina stared straight forward, not making eye contact. Cinderella watched her quietly. "You feel no remorse... do you?"

Georgina exhaled, her eyes closed. When she opened them again they appeared glassy. "I believe I have long been without such capabilities," she answered quietly.

"So you are perfectly happy with what you almost accomplished?"

"On the contrary... I feel positive things far less than I do negative," she said, still staring.

Cinderella regarded her silently, unsure of how to proceed. "What *do* you feel, Georgina?"

"...Empty," she whispered. "I have since the moment my husband died."

Cinderella felt an overwhelming rush of emotions towards her stepmother; anger, hatred, annoyance, shame, sadness, disgust, pity... but most of all, compassion. She rose from her throne, rushing down the stairs to embrace Georgina, to tell her that all was not lost, that she could do better; *be* better.

She reached the foot of the stairs when the doors were thrown open and none other than Conte Digby Baron came running in. "Asche, you mustn't do this!" he cried. "Do not execute them! Please, think of your mother!"

Cinderella was stunned at such a proclamation. "Father, I have no plans to execute *anybody*," she insisted.

Her father stopped at Georgina's side, now looking rather confused. "Oh, well I-I-"

"-Georgina... return home with my father," Cinderella said. "Go to the home I cared for all those years, with my father... and learn to *love* it." Georgina stared into her eyes as though Cinderella had gone mad.

"It is a wonderful place, a *magical* place," she insisted. "See it for what it is and not through the lens of your loss. Feel the sunlight on your face as you dig the garden beds, feel the cool tiles under your hands while you wash them, appreciate the heat of the fireplace while you make breakfast... even in the summers, for in the winters you shall miss it.

"Learn what it means to *live* again, Georgina... then, who is to know? Good feelings may return in time... laughter, appreciation... kindness... it may all very well come back to you," Cinderella finished. A guard came forward and took Georgina gently by the elbow. She allowed herself to be guided from the room.

Cinderella remained with her father. "Asche I–"

"–Cinderella."

"Pardon?"

"My name is Cinderella," she told him. "At least when I am here..."

Her father looked uncomfortable but nodded. "I understand. I have come about the war council. I only heard just as I arrived outside exactly who you were meeting with in here," he told her.

"What do you know about the war council?" Cinderella asked.

"King Sebastian claimed that the King of Nowhorl disagreed with the amendment to the Kingdom's War Treaty and as such has made them out to appear as though they are hoarding resources for themselves, for they have a large portion of their border running along the ocean, which also makes their land highly desirable due to its easily defensible nature," her father began.

"I do not understand how that connects?" Cinderella said. "Sebastian only cares about what Nowhorl did to his mother; what he *believes* they did to his mother," she corrected herself.

"He may not, but the other kingdoms most definitely do!" he went on. "At the war council he informed the courtiers that he had met with the members of each royal family to ask the same of them that he did Nowhorl; amend the treaty."

"Yes, he did."

"No... he did not."

Cinderella paused. "You... you think he lied about meeting with the other royal families?"

"I *know* he did!" her father rambled erratically. "I spent much time with them over the past few days. Not a single one of them mentioned a royal meeting and none of them disappeared for any length of time to allow such a thing!" he said. "Unless of course they were meeting in the dead of night."

"No, Father," Cinderella sighed. "The King keeps himself busy in *other* ways at night..." Her father looked disconcerted at the thought. "What are you saying? He bluffed King Linas into believing all the other kingdoms had agreed to the amendment so when he was told ex parte meetings had occurred without him and he declined as a result..."

"It would give every kingdom an excuse to lay claim on Nowhorl," her father nodded. "The war council is decided. The armies march for Nowhorl tomorrow. The royal family, as well as King Hugo, are to be executed tonight."

24

"The war council is met. It has too late!" Zarina cried. They had congregated in the royal chambers, waiting for further word. Cinderella had pulled Vladimir and Zarina from her room and out from under the watchful eyes of the guards and led them to hers, where the guards had been stationed since eight o'clock that morning. As such, they had no idea what was occurring on the floors below.

Both of them had been shaken by the revelation that Sebastian had specifically set up King Linas to be overthrown by the Continental Alliance by falsely attempting to hide a treaty amendment term in the marital contract between Vladimir and Princess Willow.

"He never cared about a marriage to bond the kingdoms at all!" Vladimir exclaimed. "He never even cared about amending the treaty!"

"He simply used it as a means to turn the other kingdoms against Nowhorl," Zarina said, pacing back and forth, her arms crossed. "The amendment would have been a perfectly reasonable request to put to the Continental Alliance as a whole if he had called a meeting."

"Instead, he met with only Nowhorl... then claimed the other kingdoms had already agreed," Cinderella continued.

"And they all want a piece of Nowhorl for themselves and are willing to turn a blind eye while the entire royal family is executed to get it!" Vladimir finished.

Zarina dropped into a chair, head in her hands as she began to sob. "We must *do something!*" she choked. "They *cannot* die!"

Vladimir pulled her head onto his shoulder. "We cannot let him do this!" she begged.

"The moment we speak out, our heads are under the guillotine as well," Vladimir said. Cinderella got to her feet and ran to her room. "Asche, what is it? What are you doing?" he called to her.

"We cannot release the royals and your father looking like this! We need to go in *disguise!*" she said, returning with a grey smock and a white apron that she never though she would ever wear again.

Vladimir approached his brother at the head of the table. The second war council had begun, this time with the other Heads of State. "Brother! Thank you for being so gracious as to wait for me!"

"I would not have you miss it!" King Sebastian noticed who was at his side and rose to his feet. "Zarina... Why have you come?"

"Regardless of my feeling for Nowhorl I am a member of the royal family and my duty is to my King and our people," she said diplomatically. "I promised that especially for the beginning of your reign I would be by your side, offering my skills as they were needed. This a war council and as such, my knowledge is absolutely necessary," she finished.

"You would see our father dead, executed for treason... to serve me?" he asked, as though deliberately provoking a response.

Zarina went red. "No, I would not," she answered, not looking away. "And I would hope that you would not expect me to witness such a thing, but I will serve this kingdom as is expected of a Princess."

Sebastian did not seem satisfied. "Even if it meant accepting a marriage that *I* saw fit?"

"My marriage was to be my choice!" Zarina exclaimed.

"*Zarina*," Vladimir admonished quietly.

Zarina looked away, the anger clear on her face. "Do I have your word any marriage would be directly beneficial to the kingdom and its people?" she asked Sebastian.

"Sister!" Sebastian exclaimed. "I could never waste such a valuable resource!"

Zarina's face burned with rage. "*I am NOT a resource to be allocated!*"

Sebastian laughed, returning to the head of the table. "Now, have a seat and let us begin! Where is Cinderella?"

Vladimir grasped Zarina's hand and forcing her silence as they took their seats. "Seeing to her stepsisters Your Majesty... in the serving quarters."

♠

Cinderella was indeed in the serving quarters seeking out her stepsisters. "Excuse me, Rita?" she said to a round freckly woman with dark brown eyes.

"Yes!" she barked. "What do you want? Hurry now, we are busy down here!"

"Of course, Madame!" she said quickly. "June and Charlotte LaBelle, Madame? They are to be taken to the Queen immediately!"

"Room four! That way!" she pointed down a corridor to her left.

"Thank you, Madame!" she nodded, disappearing as quickly as she could. Between her recent arrival at the palace and her vastly altered appearance from anything the staff had ever seen, it was as though she were a ghost. She could go anywhere, do *anything* as a maid. Cinderella grinned to herself as she walked down the corridor. It seemed Cinderella had far more capabilities than she ever thought possible.

She reached room four and knocked. The moment the door opened she pushed her way in and closed it. "I need your help!" she whispered as loudly as she dared.

"*Cinderella?*" June gasped. "What has happened?"

"Why are you dressed like that?" Charlotte asked.

"*Shh!* I will explain everything!" she said, looking over her shoulder at the door. "Have you heard about what is occurring in the palace right now?"

Charlotte shook her head. "Madame is saying there is much to do with all the royals in house? Apparently there is to be an event tonight?" June said.

"An event indeed... They are executing the former King and the royal family of Nowhorl," Cinderella told them.

June and Charlotte's jaws dropped. "King Sebastian is having his father *executed?*"

"Not if I can help it," Cinderella said determinedly. She looked them in the eyes. "Can I trust you?"

Charlotte and June glanced at each other, then nodded to Cinderella. "We have done much to atone for," Charlotte mumbled, looking at her feet.

"Quite," June agreed. "Whatever you need us to do, we shall do it."

"I need you to get down to the dungeons. Find a way to get to the royals. Find out who has the keys and steal them if you can. Tell them... tell them help is coming."

♠

Sebastian had concluded the war council and only he, Vladimir and Zarina remained when Cinderella, back in her royal finery, rejoined them. "Tell me everything! What have I missed?"

"The executions have been confirmed for seven thirty; they will be collected from the dungeons by seven, the executioner is readying the guillotine, which will be in place by five o'clock and both the courtiers and the Heads of State have confirmed their attendance," Vladimir reported factually as he sipped his tea.

It seemed as though he were merely updating her, but Cinderella received every hidden message. *The royals will be moved by seven. From five o'clock the guillotine will be in the square. Not a single member of any royal family will be missing from the attendees.*

"That was fast," Cinderella commented innocently, taking her seat and accepting the plate of food from the serving attendant.

"You will be in attendance also," King Sebastian said. It was not a question.

Cinderella pretended it was. "Of course I will! Where else would I be?"

"So your family has been dealt with?"

"Yes. June and Charlotte are now serving the palace for me, just as I served them all those years and Georgina has been returned to Baron mansion, where she will learn every inch of the place." Cinderella took a sip of her tea.

"Just as you did," Vladimir said.

"Just as I did," Cinderella agreed. "So where are we to be, Sire?" she asked Sebastian. "Are we awaiting the incoming nobles, or shall we arrive later?"

"The ushers will lead in the courtiers, then the royals of the outer kingdoms, then the inner kingdoms, then us," Zarina informed her. "There must be a *very* strict order, Brother," she said to Sebastian. "The more important you are, the later you enter, minimising the wait prior and the closer their entry is to ours. By entering last it announces to everyone else in attendance that it is *you* they are all waiting for."

Sebastian nodded thoughtfully. "You need to decide where your strongest ties will be," she told him.

"How do you mean?"

"For example, who will enter immediately before us?" she asked. "In the eyes of the nobles *they* will be considered the next highest authority. You need to order the royals with great specificity, because those you give higher authority, it is presumed you have or *wish* to have a stronger bond with," she explained.

"Jilandra," Sebastian said. "They have the mines."

"Excellent choice," Zarina nodded, making a note on her scroll. "The three top families will be considered your inner circle, so they must be chosen quite carefully. I would also recommend Holgerra."

"Why? They have very little to offer our kingdom by ways of resources and aid," Sebastian said.

"Yes, *but* the Queen of Holgerra is in fact, the *cousin* of King Ulmar of Brionah!" she informed him.

"Brionah?" Sebastian said. "Is she truly?"

"Yes! *And* her younger sister Sophia married into the Duton royal family. By including Holgerra and courting Queen Yolanda appropriately, you have the potential to solidify an alliance *six* kingdoms strong!" Zarina insisted excitedly. Not all of it was faked either; she was truly in her element when it came to political relationships.

"Zarina you *are* brilliant," Sebastian told her, shaking his head in amazement. "How could I ever have thought I could do this without you?"

"Inexperience," she answered bluntly. "Luckily you are well on your way to seeing that problem resolved."

Sebastian's face turned stormy. "Quite so," he growled.

Cinderella could feel sweat dripping down her back. The summer heat was sweltering, and she knew that a simple slip of the tongue could see them all exposed. She sat there, desperately agonising over every word while Vladimir and Zarina sat there talking away as though their father was not a single floor below them chained in a dungeon! How could they possibly? Cinderella sat there in awe of the both of them. Royal life certainly did train you in very specific skills.

Cinderella continued to stew in her own fear and growing panic, delicately sipping tea and eating her food, as much as her churning stomach would allow. Sebastian and Zarina carried on their conversation as though it were a standard day. She was so focused on taking deliberate bites of her food that she did not notice when a serving maid stopped at her side.

"May I fill your cup, Your Majesty?" she asked softly, causing Cinderella to jump, then gasp and drop a biscuit to the floor. It was Charlotte.

"Oh... Oh, yes, please. Forgive me, I was startled," she said, as Charlotte bent down to clear away the mess. As she rose back up again, she pressed a small metal rod into her lap.

Cinderella grasped it firmly as Charlotte rose back up and poured pour tea into her cup. "Think nothing of it, Majesty," she said softly, returning to her place by the door.

"Uh...My King?" Cinderella said slowly. "Shall we retire to our chambers and change? I am assuming you would need something more formal?"

"Yes, Brother!" Zarina chimed in. "Most definitely. You need something the same level as what you wore on your coronation day!"

"Why?"

"*Sebastian!*" Vladimir said, every appearance of shock as he acted so perfectly. "This is the first decision of your Kingship, the *first* royal event of your reign! You need to present yourself appropriately." He got up. "Let us find you the perfect suit."

Vladimir steered Sebastian from the room, looking back over his shoulder to Cinderella. His eyes opened wide when he saw the key she held up. "*Zarina!* Join me in my chambers, will you? I would appreciate your assistance in selecting the right gown!" she asked loudly as Vladimir and Sebastian made their way to the staircase.

"Of course, my Queen!" she said, joining Cinderella at the door.

Cinderella turned to Charlotte. "The guillotine will be in the courtyard at *five o'clock,*" she said quietly. "You and June must find a way to sabotage it!"

"I am sorry, who are you?" Zarina asked, frowning.

"This is my stepsister, Charlotte."

"Hello," Charlotte said politely.

"Cinderella we mustn't speak with *anyone!* How do we know she is trustworthy?" Zarina hissed angrily.

"Because she brought us this," Cinderella answered, raising her hand. Zarina's jaw dropped as she saw the rusted, iron key in her hand.

25

"She wants us to *what?*" June asked incredulously.

"We have to sabotage the guillotine!" Charlotte repeated. "It is going to be there already! We have to go! Now!" she began to drag her sister out of their room.

"Charlotte, wait!" June squeaked as she was pulled though the corridors. "This is more likely to get *us* executed than it is to save the others!"

"Better that than the quarries!" Charlotte said softly in a singsong voice as she peeked around the corner. "We have to do a lap of the halls that surround the courtyard and see where the guards are."

"And we get rid of them *how?*"

"I shall think of something!" Charlotte said hastily as they made their way around the courtyard at a purposeful speed, not slow enough as to appear suspicious but not so fast that they drew attention for rushing.

"Four guards," June said, eyeing off each one without moving her head. "Two at the entry to the courtyard proper and two leading into the throne room."

"Perfect," Charlotte whispered. "*Scream!*"

"*What?*"

"Scream, then run," Charlotte told her. "Keep the guards busy for as long as you can." She immediately pushed her forward, then ducked behind a suit of armour as June turned her startled cry into a full, terror filled scream.

From behind the suit Charlotte watched as all four guards took off after her. She gave them to the count of five, before running into the courtyard and climbing onto the platform that had been erected in the centre. On top sat a dangerously sharp blade inside a wooden frame.

Charlotte started fumbling with the cords along the side of the frame. She carefully unwove the cabling from the intricate mechanisms, and, keeping it taught, she retied near the top. Now, when it was released, the blade would not move... hopefully.

Below the courtyard, in the confines of the dungeon, the Nowhorl royal family and the former King Hugo were manacled in their cell.

"We have been given strict orders from the King not to allow anyone inside!" a voice came down the seeping stone steps.

"Do you really think such an order applied to *me*?" a harsh voice snapped. "This is the missive from the King, now allow me through *immediately!*"

"Yes, Your Highness!"

There were a series of taps and clicks as whoever owned the familiar voice came down the stairs. "Leave us!" Zarina ordered the guard in the dungeon room.

"Princess, I cannot leave-"

"DO YOU THINK I AM UNDESERVING OF A FINAL UNINTERRUPTED GOODBYE WITH MY FATHER?" she yelled, cowing the guard. He bowed swiftly and disappeared up the stairs.

The moment he was gone, Zarina ran to the barred door, reaching into her pocket and pulling out the key that matched the lock. "Zarina! You have to leave *immediately!*" Hugo barked.

"Father," Zarina began, fumbling with the lock. "I believe Sebastian has made it quite clear that you are not in charge anymore."

"The *nerve!*" a high female voice gasped. Queen Harriet.

Hugo merely grumbled. "I know what daughter I raised... her mother's."

"Thank you, Father!" Zarina said as the door swung open. "Now, let us get you all out of here!"

Within three seconds Princess Willow had run to the door, threw herself through it and into Zarina's arms, kissing her fiercely. Zarina threw her arms around her, kissing her over and over, laughing and crying all at once. "I was so scared I would not get to you in time!"

"What in the blazes is going on here?" King Linas barked gruffly. "Get your hands off my daughter!"

"King Linas; I am going to get you all out of here," Zarina told the King with the authority of an army general. "Then, I can *absolutely* guarantee you Sire, there is no force on earth that will ever keep me from your daughter again." She placed her hands on her hips. "So, what will it be? Are you coming or staying?"

King Linas shared an inscrutable look with Queen Harriet. She shook her head, at a loss of what to do. King Linas then groaned. "I suppose you are better than any of the other suitors that have called to court her."

Willow jumped at her father. "I love you!"

"Yes... right, well~"

"~We need to stay quiet," Zarina said as she unlocked the chains that bound her father.

"Zarina, stop," he said softly.

"What is it Father?"

"You... you must leave me here," Hugo said, not looking up from the floor.

"Are you insane? Sebastian will kill you!"

"And who gave him the opportunity, eh?" Hugo asked solemnly. "Who handed him the crown and gave him the power to destroy us all?" He shook his head. "This is my recompense... I deserve to be here."

"Hugo... you may have been a King, friend, but you have always been human," King Linas told him. "You believed giving your heir more responsibility he would come into his own and grow into a man and King like yourself. You showed faith in your child. That is not a bad thing."

"Look at where it has ended," Hugo said.

"But it has not ended at all!" Princess Willow exclaimed as loudly as she dared. "We have the chance to change this before it ends for the worst! It is only the end when we give up! We cannot do this without you, Hugo!" she continued. "You *formed* the Continental Alliance! You are the reason we have had peace for so long! The only person who can convince the other nobles of Sebastian's lies is you!"

Hugo looked up at Willow, still at his daughter's side. "And I thought Cinderella would make a decent daughter in law," he scoffed.

The tension in the courtyard was palpable. The courtiers had entered and the last of the royal families had been led in. From the moment the Holgerrans had taken their place, the families of Brionah and Duton, who had been brought in as the first royal families, began to mutter to each other darkly.

When Sebastian and Cinderella finally entered, taking their seats in their thrones. "Where is Zarina?" Sebastian asked Vladimir, forcefully keeping his face calm.

"She was... going to change, was she not, Cinderella?" Vladimir asked. "She helped you dress?"

"Yes, she did... but that was quite some time ago," Cinderella answered deliberately. "Maybe you should *go* and check on her?" she suggested.

"No. Send the guards," Sebastian ordered. "I want her found *immediately!*"

Vladimir nodded and headed for one of the guards lining the courtyard. "Your Highness!" he bowed.

"I need you to go and collect something from my quarters for m-" Vladimir was cut off, as a dozen guards traipsed in, bringing with them King Linas, Queen Harriet, Princess Willow, his sister Zarina, and carried in, bruised and bloodied, his father, the former King Hugo.

"*Your Majesty!* We seized the traitors as they attempted to escape the dungeons!" the lead guard declared, bowing before King Sebastian.

Sebastian glared right past him at Zarina. "It was all a lie," he growled. "You were never loyal to me."

"I never said I was loyal to you Sebastian," she spat. "Blind loyalty is a fallacy and worthy only of *dogs!* I am loyal to the crown, I am loyal to this kingdom and I will forever be loyal to its people!"

Sebastian leaned forward in his throne, regarding her with a hard face. "She goes first," he finally said. "TAKE HER TO THE GUILLOTINE!"

Zarina looked to the machine in terror and started fighting her captor. Cinderella searched every inch of the courtyard, looking for a specific fa-*there!* Charlotte, standing in the window of the balcony overlooking the courtyard from the second floor. Cinderella looked at the guillotine then back to Charlotte, who smiled and gave the smallest hint of a nod. Cinderella gave an inward sigh of relief, but even without the guillotine, Zarina only had so long if they did not put a stop to this.

"Rufus! You have to say something!" she called to him over the uproar. He was white as a sheet. "They will not listen to me, but they know you!"

He gave a shaky nod, then he took a running leap up onto the platform. "FRIENDS! NOBLES! WE MUST STOP THIS IMMEDIATELY!"

"Vladimir! *Get down now!*" Sebastian ordered. "Unless you also wish to join them?"

"There are fourteen kingdoms here Brother, and regardless of whose land we stand on, for the love of the land we share and the bond we made in the Continental Alliance, they should be considered just as important as the rest of us!"

"Nowhorl has already been stripped of its status!" Sebastian yelled, getting to his feet. "There are only thirteen kingdoms now! And those that remain deserve to have their lands free of *traitors!*"

"Sebastian, you targeted Nowhorl because you blame King Linas for Mother's death! They are not traitors!" Zarina cried out, still fighting the guard the held her.

"*They are murderers!*"

"YOU ARE THE MURDERER! *You* told the royal family you had met with the other kingdoms to negotiate the treaty amendment but you *never did!*"

"*That is ENOUGH!*" a deep voice boomed across the courtyard. Everything fell silent. A tall, dark skinned man in a black fur cloak stepped forward. "I am King Ulmar of Brionah!" he called to the crowd. "Things are not as they appear, King Sebastian! You claimed Nowhorl sought to undermine us! Keeping resources for themselves with the aim of eventually taking our lands!

"We were informed your father had sought to illegally reclaim the throne when you tried to put a stop to it! You promised fairness and egalitarianism, but instead of showing equality but having the royal families enter together, you played favourites, bringing in the Queen of Holgerra, my own cousin, before myself and my Queen, *despite* our cultural expectations of elder respect-!"

"-What?" Sebastian cried. "I knew nothing of your cultural expectations! I selected my inner circle based on what would make the strongest alliance! Just as Zar-"

He stopped, glaring at Zarina, who stood there with a satisfied smile, despite having one of her arms wrenched up behind her back. "Yes, Brother!" she said.

"YOU SEE?" Sebastian roared, pointing. "SHE SET OUT TO TEAR APART THE ALLIANCE!"

"You saw to that yourself," a gruff voice spoke up. Hugo was being held up by two guards, a third holding a sword to his back. The guard dug the sword in, causing Hugo to cry out in pain.

Cinderella got to her feet. "Let him speak!" she ordered.

"Be *silent!*" Sebastian ordered.

"*I would also hear him speak!*" the King of Duton yelled to the assembled crowd.

"I have spent the last three decades ruling alongside all of you," Hugo began. "Was there ever a time I gave you pause to doubt me? To question how I chose to rule my kingdom? Caused concern within our friendships?"

Silence.

"I may have made a grave error in naming my son King before his time... but I would never knowingly place the kingdoms at risk. *Please*... for everything we went through together; for the alliance that has held for *thirty years*, please, release Nowhorl. They have done nothing wrong," he concluded, panting heavily as he struggled to breathe through his injuries.

"LUDICROUS!" Sebastian yelled. "They are to pay for what they have done, just as you will! *GUARDS! TAKE HIM TO THE GUILLOTINE!*" He swung around to face Cinderella. "And *you*... you are next."

26

Two guards began to drag Hugo towards the platform as the others held back Zarina and the Nowhorl royals. Beyond them, the courtiers and other royal families began to yell, but their words were lost in the melee. "NO!" Zarina screamed. "*Sebastian you cannot go through with this!*"

Cinderella ran to her. "*STOP HER!*" Sebastian roared. She felt thrown back in time, to her untimely exists from the festival balls. *Well, that sounds eerily familiar.* She had just made it to the platform, dodging the guards as they came at her. "Catch her at once!"

"*I HAVE HER!*" Rufus yelled, taking Asche's hand and pulling her onto the platform. He then spun around, elbowing the guard who held his sister in the face and stole his sword. Zarina groaned, rubbing her sore arm. When another guard came at her Asche rushed him and as he tumbled from the platform she took hold of his sword, unsheathing it as he fell.

Zarina, Rufus and Asche stood back to back atop the platform as, all around them, chaos erupted. Courtiers were screaming about treason while the royal family called for execution; whether they meant her and her accomplices or Sebastian for his evident lies, Asche could not tell. "GUARDS TO YOUR STATIONS! THEY DO NOT LEAVE ALIVE!" Sebastian ordered.

"KINGDOMS, TAKE UP ARMS!" King Ulmar roared over him, causing the guards to pause. "There is tyranny afoot! You would murder your own family, yet you blame Nowhorl for the death of your mother? You would destroy the peace with which we have lived for so long for a selfish endeavour where there lies no blame?"

He moved towards Sebastian, drawing his own sword. The guards reacted, coming at King Ulmar, and when his son made to intervene and the guards aimed their swords at him, the scene exploded. From their places atop the platform, Zarina, Asche and Rufus watched the madness unfold. King Ulmar leapt into the fray to defend his son, while royals of every kingdom drew weapons to defend themselves against Sebastian's guards.

"*TRAITORS! TRATIORS, ALL OF YOU!*" he screamed, his crown almost comically askew. "KILL THEM ALL!"

It became a battle between the guards and every noble in the courtyard. "Zarina!" Asche heard Willow cry out.

"*Willow!*" And Zarina was gone. She leapt off the platform and into the mass of bodies all fighting to escape the guards.

Rufus turned to her. "I have to get to my Father. Stay safe," he ordered. Before she could respond he had disappeared into the crowd, fighting his way towards Hugo.

Asche waved the sword at the guards who attempted to climb onto the platform. She was almost near tears at the thought of their pain as she slashed the blade across whatever limb came near her, but she had to give Rufus time to find his father and get him back to the throne. She knew the guards were following their King loyally and she could not fault them for that, but Sebastian's forces had to be stopped or it could mean the end of the Continental Alliance and life as they knew it. *As if that has not happened already this week!*

She swung around, seeing a guard climb up behind her from the corner of her eye. He dodged her sword and parried it with a thrust of his own. It was not a guard.

Sebastian.

In her shock she stumbled back. "You will not escape, Cinderella!" he said. He struck at her with his sword again. She clumsily batted it away.

"Did no one tell you, Sire?" she asked, taking a step and lunging forward with her sword. Sebastian dodged it easily after all his years of training, but it was enough to catch him off guard. Cinderella turned to run. "My name is *Asche!*"

He caught her on the ankle. By sheer luck she was wearing a high ankle boot or she would have lost the foot entirely. Asche cried out as she fell towards the guillotine. "Thank you for such a perfect placement!" Sebastian bowed mockingly... before he swung his sword at the cord holding up the blade.

"ASCHE!" she heard Rufus yell from the crowd. She screamed as the cord fell away. When the blade did not move, she remembered Charlotte's smile and nod from before. *She did it!* Asche quickly scrambled through to the other side before such a blessing was tested again.

Sebastian had paused, looking confused at the failure of his attempt to kill her. It lasted only a second before he came at her again. Asche was ready. She seized her stolen sword and ran at the King, not allowing him time to consider his next move.

"Argh!" he yelled. A single cut along his cheek. It was enough to give his pause a moment longer. "I will see you dead for this!"

"It appears you already tried that," Asche sighed. "It seems I have someone watching over me. Have you ever heard of Fairy Godmothers?" she asked, tilting her head to the side.

He yelled again, but when he tried to run at her, he fell forward. "What the devil?" He rolled over, revealing his boot laces having been tied together. "How?"

Asche moved forward, placing her sword tip under his chin. "Magic," she answered simply, and her Queen's visage melted away, revealing a young woman wearing a simple grey dress with a white apron.

Sebastian stared. "Are you going to kill me now... *Cinderella?*"

"My name is *Asche*," she reminded him, pushing forward with the sword. He fell silent as a bead of blood ran down his neck. Silence had fallen in the courtyard as everyone, guard, courtier or royal, watched the exchange.

Asche ignored them all. She could barely see the King, her husband, in front of her. Her mind's eye was fully on her mother, whose voice rang in her mind like a clear, rich bell. *Kindness, my darling. Kindness is like magic! When you send it out into the world, it returns tenfold.*

Asche dropped the sword. It fell to the floor of the platform with a clatter, Sebastian watching it as it went. She turned to the crowd. "This Kingdom and the kingdoms it calls friend have been living in peace and harmony for decades. I refuse to deliver the first kill of a new war. We are better than this. This kingdom was better than this. Pl–"

There was a roar behind her. Sebastian had managed to get out of his tangled laces and was running at her, sword in hand. Asche stayed where she was, rooted to the spot, unable to move.

Sebastian's sword never found its mark, as at the very last moment, the Conte Digby Baron threw himself between the King and his daughter, the sword sliding between his ribs and into his heart. He dropped to the floor.

Rufus was at her side within seconds, jumping over her father's body and raising his sword to his chest. "Stand down Sebastian!" he demanded of the now unarmed King.

"Never!" he spat, knocking the sword away before launching a valley of blows at his younger brother.

Asche only had eyes for her father. "Father, how could you do this?"

"I... I am... sorry," he wheezed. "You... deserved... better."

"Oh Father, none of that matters now!" she sobbed as his skin slowly lost all colour.

"I shall... see your mother... again... I suppose... that is a... a good thing... Do you suppose... she would... ever... forgive me?"

"Of *course* she will Father!" Asche wept. "Of course she will!"

"Do... you?"

"I do Father!" she promised, holding his face and kissing his forehead gently. He gave a final shuddered breath, then Conte Digby Baron became still. "Thank you for saving me," she whispered.

Sebastian was splayed across the platform, unconscious from one of Rufus' blows. Rufus left him there and crossed to Asche's side, pulling her close to him as she rid her body of every tear it held. She cried for the loss of her father, for the marriage she never wanted, for the one she did, for all she had endured under her stepmother, for the loss of her mother... for everything. After fifteen years of emotional build up, of always being together, of always being *kind*, she finally released all of her pain, so she could finally begin to heal and just be... Asche.

27

Hugo sat, once again, at the head of the table, as was right and proper. "You have all shown great faith in me," he grumbled, still finding it difficult to speak with his injuries. He had refused to be seen to by a doctor until another meeting of the Continental Alliance had been called. "More loyalty to me and my people than it appeared my own son did."

"Hugo," Queen Harriet said softly. "Each and every one of us here owes you a great debt for what you were able to do in ending the war. All of our kingdoms have known great peace and prosperity since, and now you have saved Nowhorl from complete ruin! You have never given any of us a *reason* to doubt you Sire," she told him.

"Yes," King Ulmar grunted, nursing a black eye. "And I for one will be the first to offer my most sincere apologies for the treatment of Nowhorl. It is a shame to admit, but greed blinded me," he said, taking his wife's hand. "I saw the opportunity for growth to my own kingdom and allowed that snake to convince me of your selfishness as a means to disregard my own. Can you ever forgive me?"

King Linas nodded thoughtfully. His wrists were still purple from the bruising of the manacles from when he had been chained in the dungeons. "Big of you to admit. A lesser man would not... and I cannot be so righteous as to claim I would have done differently in your stead."

"We are far more than the Heads of State," Hugo said, leaning forward. "Far more than the members of the

Continental Alliance. We are family, and as such we should start to act like it."

"In many cases, we are!" Queen Yolanda of Holgerra chuckled, tipping her glass to both King Ulmar and King Francis of Duton.

"Indeed!" Hugo agreed. "We need less methodically planned political relationships and more open and direct dialogue between our kingdoms," Hugo continued. "Allow our kingdoms to grow and change with the times as we as rulers do... well, as *you* rulers do," he corrected himself.

"But Father," Vladimir said. "You *are* a ruler?"

"I ceased to be king the moment I gave the throne to Sebastian," he said. "And I do not believe in going backwards. My abdication stands."

"But Father I never planned on being King-!" Vladimir said, shocked by the idea.

"-Neither did I," Hugo said quietly. It was enough to silence Vladimir. "But I took the duty as it was given to me by the Viscount Issa Merlot, my father's second in command after he died... as I hope Zarina will accept it when given her by Viscount Jarvis."

The room was silent for a second, before many voices started speaking at once.

"Hugo, are you sure-?"

"-Surely you can claim the throne for yourself again-?"

"-This simply is not done-!"

"-A Queen does not rule without a King-!"

"-Why not Vladimir-?"

"-Father?" Zarina said. "Me?"

"Yes, my dear," Hugo insisted, placing a hand over hers. "You... who has dedicated her entire life to the crown and what it means to lead a country, you who have studied day after day to learn the lessons of history and the importance of the relations between all of our kingdoms. You who have behaved as a Queen should from the youngest of ages.

"You took on the mantle of Queen from the moment your mother died. You attended events with me, visited other kingdoms as my ambassador, developed charities... and spent your days assisting me in all matters of state. My dear, I am simply asking you take the title."

Zarina grinned. "I will do my best to make you proud."

"You already do."

"Well, *I* am still uncomfortable with the idea of a Queen ruling alone!" Queen Valerie of Rancor insisted.

"You are right, Your Majesty!" Zarina nodded brightly. "I shall see the issue is rectified at once!"

"*Before* the coronation?" Queen Valerie pressed.

"If she will have me!" Zarina turned to Willow and dropped to her knee. "Princess Willow of Nowhorl, you are already my Queen... Will you do me the honour of becoming my wife?"

The shocked cries were drowned out by Willow's resounding "YES!"

♠

Asche never learned what happened to Sebastian. His body had been taken from the courtyard and she had not seen it since. As she stood by Zarina's side with Rufus, listening to Zarina and Willow recite their vows the very next day in the palace chapel, she noticed that Sebastian was absent. She did not question it.

Whatever had happened to him after his bout with Rufus and killing her father; she felt comfortable knowing that it no longer had anything to do with her. Hugo had declared their marriage annulled, releasing her from her vows. "It is the least I can do," Hugo had said.

She danced at Zarina and Willow's wedding, the Prince Vladimir holding himself high and proud. He seemed happy. The idea brought Asche joy in the days to come.

She stayed by Zarina and Willow, laying out the plans she had developed for the alteration to the crime and punishment regulations, citing her reparations scheme, where people would be assigned to serve the kingdom in the same manner they had been negatively impacting it before. June and Charlotte were brought before Zarina and Willow as examples of the scheme, where they were given ladies in waiting status.

June gasped, throwing her hand over her mouth in a very un-lady-in-waiting like fashion. "Thank you, Your Majesty!" Charlotte bowed.

"I am not a Queen yet, Charlotte, but I have to say no thanks are needed," Zarina told her.

"Quite so!" Willow agreed from her wife's side. "I was told of your bravery; luring the guards away and interfering with the guillotine... My entire family owe you our lives. That is not something that can be easily repaid."

"We shall prove every day that we are worthy of such an honour!" June promised, her hands now clasped together at her lap.

"Of that I have no doubt."

The coronation of the Queens was held the afternoon following the wedding. Despite the scabs and bruises still covering his face, Hugo stood by his daughter and son as

Zarina was declared Queen, and given a deep red fur cloak, a metre long golden sceptre and the large, gilded crown never before worn by a Queen. Asche clapped and cheered with the rest of the crowd, tears in her eyes for many reasons.

At the conclusion of the ceremony, Asche made her way slowly back through the palace, taking it in one final time. "Surely you will remain here with us!" Zarina gasped, shocked to hear she was leaving.

"I *must* return home," Asche insisted. "It would cause too much confusion having a past Queen with current Queens in power. This transition has been erratic enough for the people! With Sebastian's disappearance, it is best I do the same."

"But you would make such a wonderful advisor! The perfect Viscountess!"

"I need to go home Zarina," she told her gently. "You know if ever you need me, I will be at Baron Mansion. Without my mother and father... it needs me to keep their memory alive. I could not possibly imagine my home with no one there to love it."

Zarina looked around the room. "I understand completely," she said knowingly.

Asche reached the top of the stairs that led from the entrance hall to the front of the palace. The guards bowed. "Viscountess," they greeted respectfully.

"Oh, I am not..." she sighed. "Never mind. Thank you, gentlemen." At the bottom of the stairs, she disregarded the line of royal carriages and set off on foot, down the path, through the gates and into the city... alone.

"That daughter of yours is quite special... Never met one quite like her!"

Asche approached the back of the property, passing through the fence as she had so many times before. It was odd, because she never heard anybody back there. She was the only one who ever went near the willow and hazel trees at the back of the property... and no one but her *ever* came near her mother's grave.

Asche was making her way to the hazel tree when a bright light appeared in from of her just as she passed the weeping willow. "Nixie!" she gasped.

"Hello, my darling!" she said, embracing her warmly.

"I never expected things to happen as they did!" Asche began to ramble, tears falling. "I never wanted to marry Sebastian! I loved *Rufus*! I just wanted to attend the festival! I wanted to see *him*! And now... now the kingdom i-is-!"

"-*Fine!*" her Fairy Godmother said simply. "The kingdom is in the hands of Queen Zarina and Queen Willow and the people will settle into their new normal. You cannot blame yourself for how things have turned out, and even if you could, there is very little blame to be laid. What blame there is, lies with Sebastian, not you."

"How can life simply return to normal after everything?"

Nixie smiled broadly, turning to the hazel tree and the woman sitting beneath it. "It cannot my dear, nor should it. The world is wonderous... *magical*. You should see it as such." Asche joined her as she watched. "The life you knew here will not be as it was... and that is for the better. It shows you have worked miracles... far more so than I have."

Asche was still gazing through the tree branches, trying to get a look at the stone bench beneath it and its mysterious occupant. "Who *is* that?" she asked, turning back to Nixie, but her Fairy Godmother had disappeared. Asche steeled her nerves and stepped around the hazel tree.

"And here she is! Wayward daughter returned home! Come child, sit."

"Georgina?"

<h1 style="text-align:center">28</h1>

Her stepmother was a different person from anything she had ever known. She had settled into her own routine. She would get up and work with Arina and Heidi in the kitchens preparing breakfast, which everyone would then eat together in the small dining room off the conservatory. Then she would go out and assist Gerry with anything the animals needed. When that was finished, she would clean an area of the house; she had even divided the mansion into sections so she could focus on one each day.

When all her work for the day was complete, she would spend any spare time prior to dinner sitting under the hazel tree, talking to Victoria Baron, about anything that came to mind. When she had first begun going all she could do was cry and apologise, now she talked about Asche, June and Charlotte, about Digby's habits that must have annoyed the *both* of them in their time. When his body was finally returned to them, both she and Asche worked diligently to bury him alongside Victoria, for surely, Georgina thought, that is what he would have wanted.

Then, they would sit there for hours each afternoon. They would take tea there as the sun was setting, joined by Arina, Heidi and Gerry, laughing and talking to Digby and Victoria as though they were still there.

It was a pleasant existence. Asche had moved into the room she had as a child on the second floor. She insisted Georgina move back into the room she had shared with

Asche's father and after much argument, she finally agreed, but only if Heidi and Gerry and Arina were given rooms on the second floor so they could all be together.

It felt as though an age had passed, but their new normal took only a few weeks. Autumn had just made an appearance in the form of lighter green to yellow leaves on the hazel tree and a slight chill just before dawn. Asche was making her way up from the kitchen just as the heat crept back into the day one morning in mid September when Heidi called out to her. "Asche, would you mind bringing the tea tray to the conservatory on your way up?" she called.

"Of course Heidi! Give me a moment!" She turned back to collect the tray from the kitchen bench and immediately came face to face with Rufus.

"Hello Your Highness," he grinned cheekily.

"I...I-I," she babbled. "I am not royalty," she finally managed. "At least, not any more."

"Let us change that, shall we?" Rufus knelt down and took her hand. "Asche... will you marry me?"

Asche smirked. "That depends on who is asking... Are you Prince Vladimir or are you Rufus?"

"Yes," he answered. "And are you Asche Mariela Baron... or are you Cinderella?"

"I suppose we are indeed both," She said as he stood back up. "It will indeed be a new experience to marry after actually being *asked*," she laughed.

Rufus' smile widened and he lifted her into his arms, kissing her over and over.

"*WHAT DID SHE SAY?*" Arina's voice bellowed down the stairs. Rufus and Asche laughed.

♠

Georgina went about her business caring for the Baron Mansion and the graves at the edge of the property. She lived out her days with a quiet dignity that she had never known before, with no expectations to be met in order to feel contented with life. She was finally at peace, happy to spend her days cleaning and waiting for visits from her daughters, who had become far more than she had ever hoped.

Both June and Charlotte were true to their word. June was granted the title of Baroness within two years, taking a place on Queen Zarina's advisory council due to her infallible skills in cultivating relationships and creating charitable organisations. She stepped into the role Zarina herself had once held for Hugo.

Charlotte, upon her appointment as a lady in waiting, took over the curation of the palace library, where she learned every book back to front, every scroll top to bottom. Zarina was never at a loss of what information she needed, for no matter the topic, Charlotte knew where to find it. It was there she met Jakka, the Prince of Duton, while he was visiting with his uncle, King Derek. They were married the following Spring.

Zarina and Willow led the kingdom into the most innovative and abundant age the land had ever known. The people thrived as they never had before under the new Continental Alliance protocols. They had agreed that all resources would be shared and traded in such a manner that every citizen within their empire would receive what they needed.

The number of charitable organisations this allowed meant the homelessness rates dropped significantly, while the number of children able to go to school jumped, as they were no longer needed at home working the family trade and the schools themselves had grown enough to accommodate them.

This had led Hugo to start his own school in the palace. He took on as many orphaned children as he could, teaching them in various subjects with the assistance of Charlotte, training them in a wide array of skills, Jakka as his second in command.

Also, instead of meetings of the Continental Alliance being on an 'as needed' basis, it was decreed that they would meet annually. Every year a summit would be hosted by a different kingdom and they would discuss all matters of state. This would guarantee that issues being face by the kingdoms would be rectified swiftly before they had the opportunity to grow into something worse.

Asche and Rufus remained at Baron Mansion, together. Every other week they would join their family for a dinner at the palace, while on the opposite weeks Zarina, Willow, June, Charlotte and Jakka would visit them at the mansion.

On one very special visit, Willow, Zarina, Hugo, Jakka and Gerry were pacing the landing of the second floor anxiously. "Do you think everything is alright?" Zarina asked.

"She will be fine, Daughter. Women have done this a time or two," Hugo assured her. "Try to distract yourself."

"Of, of course Father," Zarina said sarcastically. "Did you hear *Oh Sew Nice!* Has disappeared? I sent a messenger to that Nixie woman Vladimir demanded to see; the seamstress? The entire shop is empty! Apparently the tailor opposite was adamant she was there just yesterday!"

"That *is* odd," Willow said, and while it was most definitely interesting, it was not enough to distract them for long. Zarina's nerves and the carpet being further worn down by the incessant pacing of the group, when a short while later, there was a loud cry from behind the doors.

♠

"Oh Asche! He is simply *perfect!*" June whispered excitedly, as Nixie passed the baby to his mother.

"Whatever will you name him?" Charlotte asked as Georgina collected up the towels scattered all around the floor.

Asche looked up to Rufus and smiled. He kissed his wife on the forehead and grinned at his precious baby boy.

"Victor," they said together.

www.ingramcontent.com/pod-product-compliance
Lightning Source LLC
Chambersburg PA
CBHW070606120726
47909CB00007B/2466